Book Seven

sweep

Cate Tiernan

THE CALLING

speak

An Imprint of Penguin Group (USA) Inc.

All quoted materials in this work were created by the author.
Any resemblance to existing works is accidental.

The Calling

SPEAK
Published by the Penguin Group
Penguin Group (USA) Inc., 345 Hudson Street, New York, New York 10014, U.S.A.
Penguin Group (Canada), 90 Eglinton Avenue East, Suite 700, Toronto, Ontario M4P 2Y3, Canada
(a division of Pearson Penguin Canada Inc.)
Penguin Books Ltd, 80 Strand, London WC2R 0RL, England
Penguin Group (Australia), 250 Camberwell Road, Camberwell, Victoria 3124, Australia
(a division of Pearson Australia Group Pty. Ltd.)
Penguin Group (NZ), 67 Apollo Drive, Rosedale, North Shore 0632, New Zealand
(a division of Pearson New Zealand Ltd)

Published by Puffin Books, a division of Penguin Young Readers Group, 2001
This edition published by Speak, an imprint of Penguin Group (USA) Inc., 2008

7   9   10   8

Cover photography copyright © 2001 Barry David Marcus
Photo-illustration by Marci Senders
Series design by Russell Gordon

Produced by 17th Street Productions,
an Alloy company
151 West 26th Street
New York, NY 10001

17th Street Productions and associated logos
are trademarks and/or registered trademarks of Alloy, Inc.

Speak ISBN 978-0-14-241022-6

Printed in the United States of America

Prologue

A wolf, silver-tipped fur, ivory teeth glinting in the candlelight, padding across a dark, polished marble floor to a stone table. The room huge, black candles flickering in wall sconces. Leaves and vines in ornate plaster molding. A cougar, muscles rippling beneath a tawny pelt, bounds toward the table, golden eyes glittering. Black drapes covering tall, narrow windows. A great horned owl, its wings and talons outstretched, hovering over the stone table. The air rank with the smells of the animals. A viper coiled on the table, fangs exposed. An eagle, an enormous bear. A jaguar, tail lashing. The air crackling with dark power. An elaborate silver candlestick with black candles burning on top of an ebony cabinet. A hawk circling. An athame set with a single bloodred ruby. A jackal, a weasel, both greedy with hunger. The wolf ravenous. All closing on the great round stone table where a wolf cub lies bound, its eyes wide with terror, its small body trembling. One by one the candles gutter out. The darkness becomes thicker, complete. And the wolf cub howls.

* * *

I bolted upright, my heart hammering. I could still hear the echo of the cub's agonized scream, and the darkness around me . . . was only the darkness of my bedroom in the middle of the night. I was in my own room, in my own bed, yet the dream was still with me, vivid and terrifying.

Hunter, I need you! Without thinking I sent a witch message to my boyfriend, Hunter Niall.

I felt his instant response: On my way.

I glanced at my alarm clock. It was just past three A.M. I padded downstairs in my flannel pajamas to wait for Hunter.

It took him only ten minutes to arrive, but it felt more like ten hours as I paced the living room nervously. The nightmare wasn't even close to fading. It still seemed present, as if all I had to do was close my eyes and I'd be right back inside it.

I looked out the window as I felt Hunter approach, crunching across the crust of old snow on our lawn. His pale blond hair stuck up in spikes around his head, and my mage-sight showed me the traces of pink the cold wind had whipped into his pale, chiseled face.

"What happened?" he asked without preamble as I opened the front door.

"I had a dream." I pulled him inside, opened his coat, and buried my face against his sweater-covered chest.

He stroked my hair back from my forehead. "Tell me."

I told him, standing within the circle of his arms, speaking in a whisper so as not to wake my family. As I spoke, the images from the dream seemed to hover in the air around me, the wolf slavering, the owl's yellow eyes searching, searching. I wanted to hide from those yellow eyes, wanted to stop them from hunting me out.

Stop. It's not real, I told myself.

"I don't know why it scared me so much," I finished lamely. "It was just a dream. And I wasn't even in it."

But Hunter didn't say the comforting things people usually say. Instead he was silent a moment, tapping his fingers gently on my shoulder. At last he said, "I think I should report it to the council."

My heart contracted. "The council? You think it's that serious?"

He shook his head, his green eyes somber. "I don't know. I'm not experienced in interpreting dreams. But there are things in it that worry me—a lot."

I swallowed. "Oh," I said in a small voice.

"Morgan?" I heard my dad's sleepy voice coming from the top of the stairs. "Are you down there? What are you doing up at this hour?"

I turned quickly. "Just getting something to drink," I called. "Go back to sleep, Dad."

"You too," he mumbled.

Hunter and I looked at each other.

"I'll call you," he whispered.

I watched him disappear back into the darkness. Then I went back up to my room and lay there, sleepless and full of dread, waiting for the dawn to come.

1
Prophecies

March 2, 1977

I dreamt of Ireland again. As always, the dream left me with a longing that makes no sense. It's just an image, deceptively simple, innocent really: a small child's dress of cream linen, blowing on a line against an open blue sky. Behind it the grass slopes up to the base of Slieve Corrofin, with the great rock at the peak in the shape of a lizard's head. I remember the locals calling it the Ballynigel dragon, though I reckon that was more for the tourists than anything else.

So why does Ballynigel still haunt my dreams? And what do I make of the fact that the dream returns when I am eighteen, two nights before I'm to marry Grania? If, as we are taught, everything has meaning, then what does this mean? Am I being warned away from the marriage? No, that seems impossible. I've been dreaming of that dress since I was eight.

Besides, Grania is three months pregnant with my child. And she's a good match. Her family is one of the wealthiest in Liathach, our coven. More to the point, her mother is the high priestess of Liathach and has no other children, and Grania has no ambition to lead the coven herself. She's happy to let me take that role. I've always known that one day Liathach would be mine to lead. Being Greer MacMuredach's son-in-law will make the passing of power that much easier. Together Grania and I will raise a dynasty full of true Woodbane magick.

—Neimhidh

At eight-thirty the sky still held the paleness of early morning as I drove south on the New York State Thruway. There were almost no other cars on the road, and the world seemed still and hushed in the chill January air. In the back-seat of Das Boot, my enormous '71 Plymouth Valiant, Bree Warren, Robbie Gurevitch, Raven Meltzer, and Hunter's cousin, Sky Eventide, were crammed together. All were sleep-ing—Raven half collapsed against Sky, Bree snuggling with Robbie. The only other person awake was Hunter, who sat in the passenger seat beside me. I glanced at him, saw his chiseled profile intent as he studied a map. Sometimes I won-dered if Hunter ever lived a moment without that focused intensity. Did he even sleep intensely?

Maybe I would find out over the coming weekend. The six of us were about to spend four nights in New York City. I'd never spent that much time with Hunter, and something deep inside me thrummed with pleasure at his being so close to me. Things were still new between us, but I knew without question that I loved him. Most of the time I felt pretty certain that he loved me, too, although sometimes I got insecure about that. I had told him how I felt weeks ago, but he had never said it back to me. Who knew—maybe he just didn't feel it was necessary. I hadn't had the nerve to ask him.

"Morgan, you'll need to take the Palisades Parkway to the George Washington Bridge, then get the Harlem River Drive to the Franklin Delano Roosevelt motorway," he said, sounding very British.

"We call them *highways* here," I said, unable to resist ribbing him.

"The *highway*, then. It will take us straight down the east side of the city."

"I know." I'd never driven to New York City before, but I'd gone with my family plenty of times. From Widow's Vale, about two hours north, it was a pretty direct route.

"How fast are you going?"

I glanced at the speedometer. "Seventy-five."

He frowned. I smiled. Responsible Hunter. At nineteen, he was the youngest member of the International Council of Witches, a Seeker, charged with ferreting out witches who used their power inappropriately and administering punishment. It was a serious job. Too serious, I sometimes felt. Since I'd met Hunter, I'd seen more of Wicca's dark side than I cared to.

About two months earlier I'd learned that I was in fact not the biological child of the people I'd always thought of as my parents. Rather, I was adopted and a blood witch, the descendant of one of the Seven Great Clans of Wicca. What's more, I was heir to an incredible legacy of power.

Magick had brought me searing grief. It had made me question absolutely everything I'd ever believed to be true. But magick was also the most amazing gift: an opening of the senses, a surfacing of ancestral memories, an exhilarating connection to the earth, and a strength I'd never imagined possible. And it had brought Hunter into my life. Hunter, who I loved more than I'd thought possible.

"You're almost up to eighty," Hunter said, sounding disapproving.

I slowed down to sixty-five. "There's no one else on the road," I pointed out.

"Except perhaps a police officer," he warned. I felt his green eyes on me, and when I glanced at him, he smiled. "Pity we don't travel by broomstick anymore," he said.

"Did we ever?" I asked, honestly curious. "It sounds like fun."

Hunter shrugged. "Really? I suspect it would be awfully uncomfortable—hard seat, no heat or air-conditioning, bugs constantly flying into your mouth. . . ."

I glanced at him again and saw the glint of amusement in his eyes. I felt a rush of delight that made me break into a goofy grin. "I guess I'll stick to driving for now."

We rode in silence for a while. The haze of thin clouds in the sky was starting to burn off, the sky settling into the pale, crystalline blue so typical of winter skies. There were a few more cars on the road now.

Hunter was the reason we were all going to New York City. Hunter, my dream, and the ancient boiler in Widow's

Vale High, which had broken down the Wednesday before Martin Luther King Jr. Day, miraculously extending a three-day weekend to five days.

As it turned out, the council had taken my dream very seriously. They considered it a prophetic vision and had ordered Hunter to investigate. "They think the animals in your dream were actually members of a Woodbane coven called Amyranth," Hunter had told me when he'd gotten the council's directive.

"Amyranth?" I frowned. Where had I heard that name before?

Of the Seven Great Clans, the Woodbanes were known for their tendency to covet and abuse power. But there were also Woodbane covens, like Belwicket, the one my birth parents had belonged to, that had forsworn evil.

"Amyranth is not one of the good ones," Hunter told me. "It's one of the worst. It's the only coven believed to practice the forbidden magick of shape-shifting. Actually, another coven, Turneval, also used to shape-shift. But Turneval was disbanded in the early seventies, after their core members were stripped of their magick by the council. Amyranth has avoided the same fate by operating in deep secrecy. Members usually maintain membership in another coven; Amyranth is their secret coven." He gave me a sideways look. "Selene Belltower was a member of Amyranth."

"Oh." *That's* where I'd heard the name Amyranth before. I shuddered involuntarily at the thought of Selene. "So we're talking very scary."

Hunter had been sent to Widow's Vale last fall to ferret out a group of Woodbane witches who were using dark magick to destroy their opponents and increase their own power. Their local leader had been Selene Belltower, the mother of Cal Blaire, Hunter's half brother and my first love. Though I was Woodbane myself, Selene had wanted to drain me of my power, and she'd used Cal to get to me. When that plan had failed, Selene had kidnapped my younger sister, Mary K., forcing Hunter and me into a horrible showdown with her, just before Christmas. She'd nearly killed Hunter and me both, and I worried that Mary K. might still be suffering some subtle bad effects from having been her captive.

Cal had stepped in front of me and taken the bolt of dark energy she'd aimed at me. Now Cal was dead, killed by his own mother. Although he'd used and betrayed me, in the end he'd given his life for me. I was still coming to terms with that: both with the fact that the beautiful boy I'd loved so much was gone and that he was gone because of me.

Selene had also died that night—and though I certainly hadn't meant to kill her, I was haunted by the fear that my magick had somehow contributed to her death. I'd never seen death up close. It was so final and empty and awful. Seeing Cal and Selene alive one minute, dead the next had changed something inside me. For all of Selene's and Cal's formidable powers, they were as mortal as anyone else. Ever since that night I'd looked at everyone I knew and loved with a new awareness. We were all so fragile, all capable of being so easily extinguished. I couldn't help thinking of that again as I drove on this beautiful morning.

"Are you all right?" Hunter asked softly. "If you grip that wheel any more tightly, you're going to wrench it off the steering column."

"I'm fine." I forced my hands to relax.

"Are you thinking about Selene and Cal?" Hunter guessed. He was very sensitive to my emotions. No one had ever read me with such precision. Sometimes it made feel vulnerable and exposed. Sometimes it was weirdly comforting. At that moment it was a little of both.

I nodded as we whizzed past an exit. No love had been lost between Hunter and Cal. They'd never known each other except as enemies. But Hunter knew I'd loved Cal and was doing his best to be respectful of that. More than anyone, he understood how much coming into my powers had cost me.

"Let's talk about something else," I said. "Can we go over the details of this vision one more time? I'm still not clear on what it is we're supposed to do."

"*We're* not supposed to do anything," Hunter said. "You're staying out of this. I don't want you taking any risks, Morgan."

I felt a prickle of annoyance. We'd had this argument several times in the two days since the council had contacted Hunter. Because I was the one who'd had the dream, the council had asked that I accompany Hunter, just in case he needed to consult with me. I, of course, wanted to go. It was my dream, after all. Besides, I loved the idea of spending time in the city with Hunter.

Hunter hadn't been so keen on the idea, though. "It's too dangerous," he'd told me flatly. "For you of all people to go walking into a nest of Woodbanes . . ."

He explained that the council believed Selene had been acting on behalf of Amyranth; it was possible I still was a target. I couldn't pretend that prospect didn't frighten me. But

Selene was dead now, nothing bad had happened to me in the weeks since her death, and I was starting to feel safer. Safe enough that my desire to go with Hunter outweighed my fear.

"The council thinks I should go," I'd argued.

"The council are a bunch of—" He broke off, pressing his lips together in irritation. My eyes widened. Was he really about to bad-mouth the International Council of Witches?

"They don't always consider the risk to individuals," he said after a minute. "They're not out here, doing the legwork. Anyway, you can't go," he went on. "You've got school. Your parents aren't going to let you take two days off to go down to the city just because a bunch of witches in London think you should." He was right about that, I had to admit.

But then the school boiler had broken down, and Bree had suggested that we combine Hunter's mission with a road trip to her dad's New York City apartment. After a long discussion my parents had said I could go, and after that even Hunter couldn't come up with any more good reasons for me not to. I smiled, thinking about it. It must have been fate.

By late Wednesday night our road trip had expanded to include six members of Kithic, our coven. Sky was coming along because she and Hunter, who were cousins, always looked out for each other. Raven wanted to be with Sky, and Robbie had come to be with Bree.

Traffic thickened as we headed down the Palisades Parkway toward the George Washington Bridge. I slowed. "So the animals in my dream were actually Amyranth witches in their animal forms—have I got that right?"

"Right," Hunter confirmed. "We think so. We know they use animal masks in some of their darker rites. It's rarer for a witch to actually be able to take on animal form, but they are capable of that as well. The council thinks that the wolf cub on the table must represent the child of the witch who appeared as the wolf."

My mouth fell open. "But—I mean, it looked like the cub was about to be sacrificed. Are you saying a mother—or father—is out to kill their own child?"

Hunter nodded. "That's the theory," he said quietly. "The most likely scenario is that the victim's power is going to be drained. Which usually means death."

"What else?" I asked after a moment, trying to match his calm.

"Well, now we get to what the council doesn't know," Hunter said. "First of all, we aren't sure which cell of Amyranth is planning this event."

"How many cells are there?"

Hunter blew out a long breath. "Four that we know of. One in San Francisco—that was Selene's group—one near Glasgow in Scotland, one in northern France, and one in New York City. We've managed to get spies into the other three cells, but unfortunately, the one in New York is the one that the council knows the least about. Basically, all we know is that it exists. We don't know the identity of any of its members, can't even connect it to any specific incidents of dark magick. It's the most shadowy of all the branches."

I tried to make sense of all of this. "So the council doesn't know who the wolf really is."

"Or who the cub is," Hunter said. "We believe that he or she is a young witch in terrible danger. But we have no idea who this witch is or why he or she has been chosen as a victim."

"And your job?" I asked.

"As I said, we've already got agents inside the other three Amyranth cells, who will find out as much as they can," Hunter said. "Since we have so little information about the New York coven, I'm to try to fill in the gaps, find the witch who's targeted, and, if it turns out the target is here in New York—"

"We've got to find a way to protect him," I said, finishing his sentence.

"*I've* got to find a way to protect him," Hunter amended. "*You've* got to relax and enjoy the city. Shop, see museums, eat bagels, visit the Statue of Liberty."

"Oh, come on. You're going to need help," I argued. "I mean, you've got nothing to go on. Where do you even begin to find this stuff out? Can we scry or something?"

"Don't you think the council has already tried all the methods of getting information by magick?" Hunter asked gently. "We're at a dead end. It's a matter of legwork now. And you can't help me on this." He laid his fingers gently on my lips as I started to protest. "You know it as well as I do, Morgan. It's simply too dangerous for you." He looked troubled. "Which reminds me of the other thing the council couldn't figure out."

"What's that?" I whacked the horn impatiently. Traffic had slowed to a crawl, even though we were still miles from the exit for the bridge.

"We don't know why you're the one who was given this dream."

A cold finger of fear traced its way down my back. I swallowed and was silent.

"Gurevitch, get your elbow out of my ribs," Raven murmured. There was a general stirring in the back, then Robbie leaned over the blue vinyl bench seat. "Morning," he said to us. "Where are we?"

"About five miles north of the city," Hunter answered.

"I'm starving," Robbie said. "How about we stop for breakfast?"

"I brought muffins," Bree announced. I glanced in the rearview mirror and saw her holding up a large white paper bag, managing to look both sleepy and cover-girl beautiful. Bree was tall and slim, with dark eyes and sleek, mink-brown hair. She and Robbie, our good friend since elementary school, had recently started going out—sort of. Robbie was in love with Bree, but when he'd told her that, she'd gotten "all squirrelly," as Robbie put it. Yet she continued to see him. What, exactly, she felt for him was a puzzle to me. Not that I was any expert on coupledom. Hunter was only the second guy I'd gone out with.

"Got any lemon poppy seed?" Raven asked as she rooted through the muffin bag. "Want one, Sky?"

"Yeah, thanks," Sky said, yawning.

Sky and Raven were a study in contrasts. Sky was slim, pale, blond, with a penchant for androgynous clothing and a delicate beauty that belied her considerable power. Raven, Widow's Vale's resident goth girl, favored a bad-girl wardrobe that left very little to the imagination. Her current outfit featured a tight black vinyl bustier that revealed the circle of flames tattooed around her belly button. A purple stud in her nose flashed as she turned her head. The interesting thing was that Raven, who had set a record for seducing guys, was now seeing Sky. And Sky was in love with Raven. It was definitely an attraction of opposites.

Hunter took a cranberry muffin from Bree and fed me a chunk of it as I navigated the torturous bridge traffic. "Thanks," I mumbled through a sticky mouthful, and he reached out to wipe a crumb from the corner of my mouth. Our eyes met and held, and I felt the blood rush to my cheeks as I saw the desire in his gaze.

"Um, Morgan?" Robbie said from the backseat. "The road is that way." He pointed through the windshield.

Still flushed, I wrenched my attention back to the road and tried to ignore what being so close to Hunter was doing to all my nerve endings. But I couldn't help wondering what it would be like to stay with him in Bree's father's apartment.

Mr. Warren was a successful lawyer with clients in the city and upstate New York. I knew his city apartment was in the East Twenties. Even if we weren't going to have the place to ourselves, being in a New York City apartment with Hunter seemed wildly romantic. I pictured us in the master bedroom, gazing out at a night view of the Manhattan skyline.

And then what? I asked myself with a twinge of alarm. Hunter, sensing it, took his hand off my thigh. "What's wrong?" he asked.

"Nothing," I said quickly.

"Are you sure?"

"Um—I'm not really ready to talk about it," I said.

"Fair enough." I could feel Hunter deliberately turning his senses away from me, leaving me to examine my own thoughts in peace.

Cal had been my first boyfriend. He'd been so beautiful, so charismatic and seductive. Not only that, he'd introduced me to magick and all its beauty. He'd told me we were *mùirn beatha dàns*, soul mates. And I'd wanted to believe him. Every fiber of my being had wanted to be with him, yet I hadn't felt ready for the final step of going to bed with him. Now I wondered if part of me had known all along that Cal was lying to me, manipulating me. It made my grief for him into a more complicated thing, layered with resentment and anger.

But Hunter was different. I loved him, trusted him, and was completely, soul-shakingly attracted to him. So why did it scare me to think about actually sleeping with him? I glanced in the rearview mirror, studying my friends. Robbie was a virgin like me, but I was pretty sure that wouldn't last long, now that he and Bree were together. He wanted her desperately. I didn't know about Sky, but I knew that Bree had lost her virginity in the tenth grade, and Raven—well, I couldn't imagine Raven *ever* being a virgin.

What was wrong with me, that I was seventeen and still so inexperienced?

"You'll want to take the next exit," Hunter murmured, and I was grateful for the gentle prompt. I merged into the traffic on the Harlem River Drive, and we swept across the top of Manhattan to the FDR Drive and the East River.

Quite suddenly the open view of the winter sky disappeared. The air became tinged with gray, and billboards and tall brick projects rose to my right. The traffic, already slow, became stop and go; impatient drivers leaned on horns. A van in front of me spewed a cloud of black exhaust. I caught a glimpse of lead-gray river water to my left, with industrial buildings on the far side. A taxi driver yelled unintelligibly at me as he passed on the right.

I felt a surge of raw, boisterous energy. We were in the city.

2

Searching

March 3, 1977

    My wedding garments are laid out. The white robe embroidered in gold with the runes to summon power. The belt woven of gold and crimson threads. The groom's wristbands, beaten gold set with rubies, that I inherit from Grania's father. Everything is spelled with charms for strength and fertility, with protections against whatever might harm us, with blessings for wealth and long life.

    I wonder about love, though. Grania teases me, saying that nothing truly touches my heart, and maybe she's right. I know I don't love her, though I'm fond of her.

    Yet my mind lingers on last summer's fling with that American Woodbane, Selene. Now, I know that wasn't love, but Goddess, it *was exciting, the most intense experience I've ever had. And that includes all the times I've been with Grania. Still, Grania is a pretty thing and very pliant. And she's strong in her magick. Our children will be powerful, and that's the most important thing. Power. Woodbane power.*

So why do I hesitate as I prepare for our wedding? And why do I keep dreaming of that damned white dress?

—Neimhidh

Bree's father's apartment was on Park Avenue and Twenty-second Street. Bree gave directions, and I maneuvered Das Boot off the FDR, across Twenty-third Street, and finally onto Park and into the garage beneath the building.

The garage attendant gave me a strange look as we pulled in. With its two front quarter panels covered with gray body filler, its slate blue hood and shiny new metal bumper, Das Boot was not looking its most sophisticated.

Bree cranked down her window and spoke to the guard. "We're guests of Mr. Warren in apartment thirty-sixty," she said. "He's arranged for a guest pass."

The guard checked a computer screen and let us in. The garage was filled with BMWs, Jags, Mercedes, and top-of-the-line SUVs.

I patted Das Boot on its piebald fender. "You're good for this place," I told it. "They need to see how the other half drives."

"It's the perfect city car," Robbie assured me. "No one would ever try to steal it."

Loaded down with bags, we walked to the elevator. Bree

hit the button for the thirtieth floor, and I felt Hunter clasp my hand. This was so glamorous, like something in a movie.

Raven smiled at Sky. "This is very cool. I love the city."

Sky smiled back at her. "Think I could persuade you to visit the Cloisters?"

"Hell, yes," Raven said. "It's a medieval museum, right? I love that stuff."

The elevator opened, and we walked down a narrow hallway to the apartment at the very end. Mr. Warren opened the door before we knocked. Like Bree, he was tall, slender, and very good-looking. He was dressed in an elegantly tailored suit and silk tie.

"Come on in," he said. He pointed to a little video monitor by the door that revealed the thirtieth-floor hallway. "I saw you arrive." He pecked Bree on the cheek, then gave me a smile. "Hello, Morgan. Haven't seen you in a while."

"Hi, Mr. Warren," I mumbled. He had always made me a little nervous.

He hit a button, and the scene on the monitor switched to the garage. Another button showed us the building's lobby and doorman. "I've told the security people that you'll be here through Monday," he said. "Did you have a good trip?"

Bree stretched. "Perfect. Morgan drove. I slept most of the way. Oh, Dad, you've met Robbie, Raven, and Sky. And this is Hunter Niall, Sky's cousin. I've mentioned him to you."

I wondered what, exactly, Bree had told her father. Did he know that Hunter and Sky were witches, that his own daughter practiced Wicca? Probably not, I decided. Mr. Warren was a pretty hands-off parent. Half the time he was in New

York City instead of Widow's Vale, and even when he was home, Bree didn't have a curfew, didn't have to be home for dinner by a certain time, didn't have to call to say where she was. My parents had been a little leery of letting me come on this trip because of that.

Mr. Warren glanced at his watch. "I'm afraid I've got to run, kids. Meeting. Bree, I've left a couple of extra keys in the kitchen. Show everyone around and help yourself to whatever's in the fridge. You can sleep anywhere except my room. I've got a dinner out on Long Island tonight, so I won't be back until quite late." He brushed her cheek with a kiss and reached into the hall closet for his coat. "Enjoy the city!"

When he was gone, Bree smiled and said, "Come on, let me give you the grand tour."

The grand tour took all of two minutes. Mr. Warren's apartment consisted of a decent-size living room whose windows looked out over Park Avenue, a master bedroom, a small study, an even smaller guest room, a bathroom, and a tiny efficiency kitchen.

Everybody *oohed* and *aah*ed, but I couldn't help feeling disappointed, and I suspected the others did, too. Bree had told us the apartment had only two bedrooms, but somehow I'd expected something bigger, grander. Privacy was going to be tough.

"Nice," Robbie said at last. "Great location."

"One bathroom?" Raven sounded incredulous. "For seven of us?"

Bree shrugged. "It's Manhattan. Space is at a premium. Actually, this place is huge by Manhattan standards."

"I like the decor," Sky said. "It's simple."

That was an understatement, I thought. Like the Warrens' Widow's Vale house, the apartment was austere. The walls were white, the upholstery, muted neutrals. The furniture was light and spare, with an L-shaped couch, a coffee table, and a flat-screen TV the only furniture in the living room. One painting hung on the north wall, an abstract block of brown fading into tan against a white canvas. There were no knickknacks, no photographs or vases. The room didn't feel very lived in.

We dropped our bags in a pile next to the couch. Hunter stood by the windows. In faded jeans that hung loose on his hips and an oversize wheat-colored sweater, he looked vaguely bohemian and wholly beautiful. The light made his eyes turn a deep jade. In the time that I'd known him, I'd spent an inordinate amount of time thinking about Hunter's eyes. Sometimes they were the color of spring grass, sometimes the color of the sea.

"What's the plan, then?" Sky asked Hunter.

"It's just after ten," Hunter said. He hadn't bothered to check a clock. His witch senses included an uncanny sense of time. "I need to call on some people," he went on. Briefly he explained his mission to the others.

"Oh, right," Raven said sarcastically. "No problem."

"Hey, I lost a needle in a haystack last week," Bree chimed in. "Think you could find that for me? You know, when you've got a second."

"Do you want help?" Sky asked Hunter quietly, and I had to suppress an irrational surge of jealousy. She's his cousin, I reminded myself. They look out for each other.

Hunter glanced at me with a very slight smile, and I knew

he'd noticed my reaction. "No," he told Sky. "Not for this part of it, anyway. It will be easier for me to get people to talk if I'm on my own. We'll meet back here before dinner. Say, six o'clock?"

"Works for me," said Raven. "There are some stores near St. Mark's Place I want to check out. Anyone want to come?"

Sky, Bree, and Robbie signed on for the St. Mark's excursion. I decided to stay at the apartment, my excuse being that I wanted to rest for a bit after the drive. Actually, I had a secret mission of my own in the city. I needed to come up with a plan of action.

When the others had left, I went to the wide double window that looked out over Park Avenue. I could feel the city humming beneath me, people in cars and buses and taxicabs; pedestrians and bicycle messengers. I felt a twinge of regret that I wasn't down there on the streets with the others. But I had work to do.

I opened my backpack and took out a book bound in dark red cloth and a dagger with an intricately carved ivory handle. They were part of my inheritance, the Book of Shadows and the athame, or ceremonial dagger, that had belonged to my birth mother, Maeve Riordan. The rest of her witch's tools were back in Widow's Vale, hidden in my house.

I settled myself on Mr. Warren's living room floor and opened the Book of Shadows to an entry dated April 1982, a few months after Maeve and Angus Bramson, my birth father, arrived in America. They'd fled Ireland when their coven, Belwicket, was destroyed by something called the dark wave, a deadly concentration of dark energies. Maeve and Angus were the only survivors.

With nothing left in Ireland and a clear sense that they were being hunted, Maeve and Angus came to New York City. Eventually they left the city and settled upstate, an hour or two north of Widow's Vale, in a tiny town called Meshomah Falls.

The entry on the page I'd turned to talked about how unhappy Maeve was in her Hell's Kitchen flat. She felt Manhattan was a place cut off from the pulse of the earth. It made her grief for all she'd lost that much sharper.

I held the athame to the page covered with Maeve's handwriting. Slowly I passed the age-worn silver blade over the blue ink, and as I did, pinpricks of light began to form a different set of words entirely. It was one of Maeve's secret entries.

I have been staring at this gold watch for hours, as though it were a gift from the Goddess herself. I never should have brought it with me from Ireland. Oh, it's a beautiful object, passed down through the ages from one lover to another. Were I to cast my senses, I know I could feel generations of love and desire radiating from it. But it was given to me by Ciaran. If Angus ever saw it, it would break him.

Ciaran gave it to me the night we pledged ourselves to each other. He said that if you place it beneath the house, the tick of the watch will keep the hearts beating within steady and faithful. Is my holding on to it a selfish hope that Ciaran somehow will find his way back into my life? I must not even think such thoughts. I've chosen to live my life with Angus, and that's all there is to it.

Next month Angus and I will leave this dreadful city for a new home upstate. I must end this heartsick madness now. I can't bring myself to destroy the watch, but I won't take it, either. Angus and I will move on. The watch will stay here.

Ciaran had been Maeve's *mùirn beatha dàn*, but he had lied to her, betrayed her. And then, years later, long after she'd rejected him, he had found her and Angus in Meshomah Falls, where he'd trapped them in an abandoned barn and set fire to it. She was pure goodness, he pure evil. How could she have loved him? It was unfathomable. Yet . . . yet I'd loved Cal, who had nearly killed me the same way Ciaran killed Maeve.

I needed to know more. I needed to understand, as much to silence my questions about myself as to know Maeve more fully.

When we'd made the plan to come to New York, it had dawned on me that while we were there, I'd be only a subway ride from where Maeve and Angus had lived. If I could find their apartment, then maybe, just maybe, I'd find the watch. Maeve had said she was leaving it behind, after all. I knew the odds were heavily against its still being there—it had been almost twenty years ago, and even if she'd hidden the watch, surely someone would have found it. Still, I couldn't let the idea go. I wasn't even sure why I was so obsessed with the watch. Morbid fascination? I needed to see it, hold it.

Of course, I realized that anything touched by Ciaran was tainted, even potentially dangerous. Which was why I hadn't mentioned the watch to Hunter or anyone. Hunter would never approve of my doing anything remotely risky. But I had to try to find it.

I tucked the athame and the Book of Shadows back into my pack. At home I'd tried scrying with fire for Maeve's old Manhattan address. All I'd seen was a vision of the inside of a dingy apartment. Granted, most witches considered fire the most difficult medium with which to scry, but I had a natural connection to it, another gift from Maeve. But what the fire revealed was only a second cousin to what I asked for, close but not quite right. Was I doing it wrong?

It was doubly frustrating because just before Yule, I'd undergone a ceremony called *tàth meànma brach* with Alyce Fernbrake, the blood witch who ran Practical Magick, an occult store near Widow's Vale. *Tàth meànma* is a kind of Wiccan mind meld, where one witch enters another's mind.

Tàth meànma brach takes it one step further: it's an exchange of all you have inside you. Alyce gave me access to her memories, her loves and heartbreaks, her years of study and knowledge. In turn I gave her access to the ancestral memories that flowed through me from Maeve and her mother Mackenna before her.

I came out of the *tàth meànma brach* with a much deeper knowledge of magick. Without it I'd never have stood a chance against Selene. It had focused me, connected me to the earth so powerfully that for almost two days afterward I'd felt almost like I was hallucinating.

Since then I'd gotten more used to the infusion of knowledge I'd received from Alyce. I wasn't conscious of it all the time. It was more like I'd been given a filing cabinet chock-full of files. When I needed a certain piece of knowledge, all I had to do was check my files.

Of course, the knowledge in those files was specific to Alyce. For example, I now had a wonderful sense of how to work with herbs and plants. Unfortunately, scrying wasn't Alyce's strong point. That meant I had to resort to more mundane means to find out where Maeve and Angus had lived.

In Mr. Warren's study I found a Manhattan phone book. I got the address for the city's Bureau of Records, then consulted a subway map Mr. Warren had left out for us. The bureau was near City Hall. The number 6 train would get me there.

I'd just put on my coat and scarf and grabbed one of Mr. Warren's spare keys when the door to the apartment opened and Bree came in.

"Hey," she said.

"Hey, yourself. Where is everyone?"

"I left them in an East Village art gallery. There's some kind of performance going on involving a stone pyramid, two dancers dressed in aluminum foil, and a giant ball of string. Robbie was mesmerized," she said with a laugh. "Are you going out?"

I hesitated. I didn't want to lie to Bree, but I didn't want to tell her about my quest for Maeve's watch, either. I was afraid she'd try to talk me out of it. "I was going to run a few errands," I said vaguely. "And I thought we could use some candles for Saturday night's circle. You're sure your dad doesn't mind us having a circle in his apartment?"

"He probably wouldn't, but he'll never know," Bree assured me. "He's seeing some woman who lives in

Connecticut, and he's going out to her place this weekend."
She pulled out her wallet and checked for cash. "I'm going to
stock up on some food—if I know my dad, his idea of food in
the house is one wedge of gourmet cheese, a jar of imported
olives, and a bag of ground coffee."

Bree's prediction was accurate except for the cheese,
which was nonexistent. "Why don't we go together?" she
suggested. "I know all the good stores in the neighborhood."

"Sure," I said. I realized I was glad of the chance to spend
a little normal time with Bree, even though it would delay my
trip to the Bureau of Records.

Bree and I had been best friends since we were little kids.
That, like nearly everything else, had changed this past fall
when Cal Blaire came into our lives. Bree fell for him, Cal
chose me, and we'd had a horrible fight and stopped speaking to each other. For a hideous couple of months we were
enemies. But on the night that Cal tried to kill me, Bree had
helped save my life.

Since then we'd begun to rebuild our friendship. We
hadn't yet found our way back to being completely easy with
each other. On the one hand, she was the friend I knew and
loved best. On the other, I'd learned there were parts of Bree
I didn't know at all.

Besides, I was different now. Since I'd learned I was a blood
witch, I'd been through experiences that were both amazing
and horrifying. Once Bree and I had shared everything. Now
there was a huge part of my life she could never understand.

We walked toward Irving Place. The wind was brisk
and cold. I gave myself a moment to adjust to being on
the streets, massive buildings towering overhead, people

hurrying by. It was as if New York moved at a pace faster and more intense than the rest of the world. It felt both intimidating and wonderful.

"Pretty cool, huh?" Bree said.

"It feels like we're light-years away from Widow's Vale."

"We are," Bree said with a grin.

"So . . . things are good between you and Robbie?" I asked.

"I guess," she said, her grin fading. We went into a supermarket. Bree grabbed a basket, headed for the deli counter, and ordered macaroni salad and sliced turkey breast.

"You guess? You two seemed pretty much in sync on the drive down."

"We were," she said. She shrugged. "But that doesn't mean anything."

"Why not?"

She gave me a look that made me feel like I was seven.

"What?" I asked. "What's wrong with Robbie?"

"Nothing. We get along great. That's the problem."

We moved to the aisle with chips and sodas, and I tried to make sense of what Bree had just said. I'd seen Bree break up with dozens of guys for all kinds of reasons. One was too self-absorbed; another too controlling. One bad-mouthed everyone; another couldn't talk about anything except tennis. One guy was such a lousy kisser that Bree got depressed just looking at his lips.

"Okay," I finally said. "Maybe I'm dense, but what is the problem with a relationship in which the two people get along great?"

"Simple," she said. "If you love someone, you can get hurt. If you don't, you can't."

"So?"

"So . . . Robbie wants us to be in love. But I don't want to fall in love with Robbie. Too risky."

"Bree, that's ridiculous," I said.

She grabbed a bottle of Diet Coke and turned to me, anger flickering in her dark eyes. "Is it?" she said. "You loved Cal, and look where it got you."

I stood there, stunned. She could be so cruel sometimes. That was one of the things I hadn't really realized about her until our falling-out.

"I'm sorry," she said quickly. "I—I didn't mean that."

"You did," I said, struggling to keep my voice calm.

"Okay, maybe I did," she admitted. The hand that held the basket was trembling. "But I also meant that loving someone—really opening your heart to them—is just asking to have your heart smashed and handed back to you in little pieces. I mean, love is great for selling perfume. But the real thing, Morgan? It just trashes everything."

"Do you really believe that?" I demanded.

"Yes," she said in a flat voice. She turned and strode down the aisle.

"Bree, wait," I called, hurrying down the aisle after her.

I caught up to her at a rack full of assorted potato chips. She was staring at them with a frown, apparently concentrating on just which flavor was the most desirable.

"Is this all because of your parents?" I asked in a tactful, subtle way. Bree's parents had split up when she was twelve. It had been ugly—Bree's mom had run off to Europe with her tennis instructor. Bree had been shattered.

Now she shrugged. "My parents are just one example among many," she said. "Look, it's not really that big a deal. I'm just not into the whole love thing right now, that's all. I'm too young. I'd just rather have fun."

I could tell the subject was closed, and I felt a pang as the realization of how far apart we'd been pulled hit me yet again.

I sighed. "Listen, there's somewhere I need to go. I'll be back in a couple of hours."

Bree looked at me, and I could read regret on her face, too. Once she would have asked where I was going, and I would have invited her along.

"I'll get the candles and some salt for the circle," she said. "Sure you'll be okay on your own?"

"Yeah," I said. "I'll see you later."

3

Witch Dance

September 6, 1977

My son was born ten days ago, and I know I should be the proud, happy da. The boy is big and healthy—but Goddess, he's a loud, needy little bugger and Grania's still so fat. When will she get back to normal? And when will someone pay some bloody attention to me for a change?

Tonight, after little Kyle screamed his lungs out for three solid hours ("Poor wee thing has colic," Grania said, as if that made it bearable), I couldn't take it anymore. I went out to the pub and had myself a few pints and a good sulk. On the way home a bony old cat dashed straight in front of me and I toppled onto someone's rubbish left out for the trash man. I didn't even think about it. I muttered a spell and blasted the damn cat. I couldn't see it die, just heard its scream in the darkness. Now

I feel a fool. I know better than to vent my spleen in such a childish way.

—Neimhidh

I found my way to the Lexington Avenue subway line, bought a MetroCard, checked my route with the map posted in the station, and was soon speeding south beneath the city streets. I'd ridden the subway a couple of times before with my family. My sister, Mary K., hated it, but I loved the speed, the relentless rhythm. It felt like I was surging through the city's veins, being propelled by the beat of its heart.

I emerged from the subway at the City Hall stop. With a bit of asking around I found the Bureau of Records and the fifth-floor office where records of the city's rental properties were kept.

The air smelled of old paper, the floors of ammonia. A wooden bench lined the wall by the door. Half a dozen people sat on it, a few reading, the rest staring into space with glazed eyes and blank expressions.

I walked up to the counter at the front of the room. Behind it were stacks of shelves filled with ledgers bound in black. A clerk stood behind a computer on the counter.

"Excuse me," I began.

She pointed at a sign that said Please Take a Number. So I took a number from a dispenser and sat down on the bench next to a man with a thick mustache. "Have you been waiting long?" I asked.

"I've spent less time waiting in line at the DMV," he told me.

I took that as a yes, but since there were only seven

people ahead of me, I figured the wait couldn't be too long. I was wrong. The clerk not only moved in excruciatingly slow motion whenever she was actually helping anyone, but she seemed to need lengthy breaks between finishing with one person and calling the next.

The minutes ticked on. I tapped my fingers on my leg, trying not to let dark images creep into my mind—images of Cal being struck by the bolt of dark magick, of his body lying there on the floor of Selene's study. Since that horrible day, those pictures often came to haunt me in moments when I wasn't actively thinking about something else.

I distracted myself by reciting—under my breath—the properties of all the healing plants I knew. After that I went through rocks and minerals. Then I began counting the tiles in the floor, the cracks in the ceiling, the scuff marks on the plastic chairs. If only I'd thought to bring a book.

It was almost two hours later when my number was called. "I'm trying to find the address of an apartment that was rented by Maeve Riordan and Angus Bramson in 1982," I explained.

The clerk looked at me like I'd just asked her to sprout wings. "That's not possible," she said. "This system doesn't find apartments by the tenants' names. You give me the address, then I can tell you who lived there."

"All I know is it was somewhere in Hell's Kitchen," I said.

She tapped fuchsia nails against the counter. "Then you're out of luck," she told me. "There are hundreds of apartments in Hell's Kitchen. I can't be searching every building listing for the Bransons."

"It's Bramson and Riordan," I corrected her, trying not to

lose the few shreds of patience I had left. "Isn't there some kind of quick computer search you can do?"

She glanced at her computer. "Program's not set up that way."

I glanced at the rows of ledgers behind her. There were dates on the spines. "Do you think I could look through the 1982 books?" I asked.

"Not without a note from my supervisor, and she's on vacation for the next two weeks." The woman gave me a malicious smile. "Why don't you come back in February?" she suggested.

"I won't be here in February," I protested.

She started typing on the keyboard. I'd been dismissed.

I turned toward the door. Then I turned back again. If this woman wanted to play a power game, I decided angrily, I'd be happy to play, too. And I'd win. I hesitated only a moment, though I knew I was about to do something I wasn't supposed to do. Well, city employees weren't supposed to be totally unhelpful, either, I reasoned.

I licked my lips and glanced around. The only person still waiting on the bench was a worn-looking elderly man who dozed as he sat. He wouldn't notice anything.

I used a very simple spell, one of the first that Cal had taught me, one I had used to retrieve Maeve's tools. "I'm invisible," I whispered. "You see me not. I am but a shadow."

The spell didn't really make me invisible. It simply made me unnoticeable, trivial. When I used it, people would focus on other things instead of me. I jumped up and down a few times to see if it had worked. The clerk didn't react, so I summoned my nerve and walked behind the counter. I hesitated when I reached for the first 1982 volume. Even if the spell made me unnoticeable, I wasn't sure it would do the same for the book.

I focused on the clerk's computer. Electricity was a form of energy and, as Hunter had taught me, energy was fairly easy to manipulate. I sent out my own energy, focusing until I picked up the emanations from the motherboard. Then I sent my energy into it, forcing the electric current into a series of irregular spikes.

"Damn, what is wrong with this machine?" the woman muttered.

Quickly I flipped open the 1982 book to the addresses in the West Forties and began scanning the cramped columns. On the seventh page I found it: Bramson. 788 W. 49th Street, Apt. 3.

I glanced at the clerk's computer screen. Lines were flickering madly across it. Quietly I replaced the book and started out of the office.

The clerk looked up as she heard me open the door. "You," she said, sounding surprised. "I thought you'd left."

I smiled at her. "You were a real help," I said. "Thanks."

I hurried out, enjoying her look of blank confusion.

As I waited for the subway that would take me back to the apartment, I wondered if the clerk's computer had recovered. Even if it was permanently fried, I had no regrets. Okay, I'd used my magick on an unsuspecting person, something I wasn't supposed to do—but she'd deserved it. Besides, I hadn't hurt her.

I knew, of course, that if Hunter ever found out what I'd done, he'd be angry. But this situation had been special. Using magick to get my birth mother's address seemed justified. No real damage had been done, and I'd gotten the necessary results.

I felt good. My magick was growing stronger and more sure, and I loved it.

That evening we ate dinner at a bustling diner on lower Second Avenue. All six of us were squeezed into a booth with red vinyl seats. Hunter was on one side of me, Robbie on the other.

"So, what does everyone want to do tonight?" Bree asked.

"I've always wanted to walk across the Brooklyn Bridge," said Robbie. "It must be gorgeous at night when you can see all the lights of Manhattan."

Bree waved a dismissive hand. "Excellent way to get mugged. Besides, it's freezing."

"Actually, I've got a lead I need to pursue," Hunter said. "There's a club not too far from here, a bit of a hangout for witches, and I'm told one of the DJs might know something about Amyranth. How would you all feel about going to a dance club?"

Raven grinned at Sky. "I could live with that."

Sky nodded, Bree said, "Sounds good," and Robbie said, "Cool."

I was the only one who seemed to have mixed feelings about going. On the one hand, I was dying to go to a cool New York club, especially one where other witches hung out. But on the other, I was terrified I'd be rejected at the door, or if I actually got in, everyone would know I was from the boonies. Besides, I've always been too self-conscious to enjoy dancing.

"I have one condition, though," Hunter went on. "If we go to this club and someone asks where you're from, just say upstate. Also, no one says anything about Selene and Cal. I don't want any of you associated with what happened to them."

Raven made a face. "Do you have to get all cloak-and-dagger on us?"

I saw Sky stiffen. Hunter, though, merely said, "We don't take risks with each other's safety." His voice was quiet but firm.

Raven looked away. "Forget I said anything."

"Fine," Hunter agreed, and let the subject drop.

The club was in the East Village, just beyond Avenue C. On the way over, Hunter hooked his arm through mine, and I felt absurdly happy. When we reached Avenue C, he nodded toward a large industrial building with big, opaque glass windows. "That's it," he said.

A husky guy in black jeans and a black leather jacket stood in front of a rope at the door. I was suddenly nervous again. "What if they don't let us in?" I asked.

"They'll let us in," Hunter said with the assurance of the effortlessly beautiful.

It occurred to me that I was the only one in our group who might have trouble. Bree was gorgeous, and Robbie was, too. Raven definitely made a fashion statement. As for Hunter and Sky, in addition to their luminous blond hair, fine, even features, and cheekbones to die for, they had a certain indefinable cool. I'm not ugly or anything, but I don't stand out, either. My hair, which I actually like, was in a single, messy braid. Plus I'd dressed for the cold, not a trendy club.

But the time for worrying was over. We were suddenly at

the door and the bouncer was opening the rope for us, with a nod to Hunter.

I felt a burst of triumph. I almost blurted, I did it. I got in! Oh God, I thought, I'm such a nerd.

"I didn't realize you were the club type," I said to Hunter.

"I'm not," he assured me with a smile as we walked into an enormous room. Near the door was a bar that opened onto a vast dance floor where two DJs were spinning house music. At the far end of the room I saw an area with cozy bench seats. Hunter pointed to it. "The café serves cappuccino and pastries. Want something?"

I shook my head. "Not yet."

We checked our coats. I gazed at my clothes doubtfully. Faded brown cords, one of my dad's oversize wool sweaters, heavy, winter hiking boots. Clearly I hadn't been thinking straight when I'd packed for this trip.

"There's someone I need to talk with," Hunter said in my ear. "Do you mind if I leave you on your own for a few minutes?"

"No, of course not," I said, though I did mind. I was feeling more insecure and provincial by the second.

Hunter blended into the crowd. I tried not to feel irked by the fact that Sky went with him, no questions asked. I stood there, trying to look casual and feeling completely out of my element.

I walked back to the edge of the dance floor. In an effort to stop focusing on my insecurities, I opened up and let my senses explore.

There was a thick, throbbing feel to the air. After a moment I realized it wasn't just the music—the club was actually pulsing with magick. I'd never felt anything like it before. There must be dozens of blood witches here, I thought. I could pinpoint a few of them even in this crowd, not so much because of what they were doing, but because power streamed out from them in a way that was almost tangible.

Most of the blood witches I knew must keep their power damped down, I realized suddenly. But not these people. Not the tall, thin African American man with the shaved head who stood on a low stage, dancing. The skinny kid in the oversize green suit. The sleek, blond woman in the low-cut, slithery dress and her dance partner, a rangy, loose-limbed guy with a beard. I frowned. Wow. There seemed to be some kind of weird psychic duel going on between the two of them. I could practically see the crackling energy that passed between them. Another woman, with long gray hair and the most extraordinary amber jewelry, danced by herself. She was sur-rounded by an aura of deep, vibrant green—it was so strong that I wondered if even those who weren't blood witches could see it.

Cal came to my mind again, unbidden. He would have loved this, I thought sadly, all these beautiful witches using their mag-ick so freely. He would have felt at home here.

Robbie came up to me, looking slightly stunned. "Is it just me, or is there something weird in the air here?" he shouted over the throbbing drums and bass.

Well, that answered my question. "It's not you," I told him. "It's magick. A lot of these people are blood witches."

"I think I'm a little out of my depth," he murmured.

"Me too," I admitted. Seeing the downcast look on his face, I asked, "Where's Bree?"

Robbie gestured silently toward the café. I spotted Bree talking to a tall, handsome man with copper-colored hair. As we watched, she turned to a younger guy, maybe seventeen or so, and with a hand on his arm she drew him into the conversation, giving him a teasing smile.

Robbie groaned. "Tell me the truth, Morgan. Am I a masochist or simply out of my mind? I mean, why do I even bother?"

"I know it looks bad," I said, trying not to get angry at Bree, "but I really don't think it means anything."

"Well, it feels awful," Robbie said. "It—" He was cut off when a girl wearing body glitter, a gold sports top, and tiny little gold shorts took his hand. "Dance with me?" she asked.

Robbie gulped, nodded, and let himself be led out onto the dance floor.

My senses were wide open now, trying to process the stunning array of magick. One guy in particular caught my eye. He was probably nineteen or twenty, with a muscular body and glossy, dark brown hair that fell to his shoulders. He was heading toward Raven, who stood near me, and there was something reckless and confident in his eyes. He wasn't exactly gorgeous, but he was very sexy. And I could sense his power from yards away. He was strong.

Then, to my shock, he stopped in front of me. "Don't I know you from somewhere?" he asked with a frown.

Was that a pickup line? I wondered, slightly panicked. Or did he really know me? Come to think of it, there was something vaguely familiar about him, too. . . .

"Um—I've never been here before," I said cautiously.

"Hmmm. Well, stop looking so impressed," he said with a

grin. "These New York witches all think they're so hot. It's not healthy to encourage them. Besides"—his eyes raked me appraisingly— "I reckon you're worth the lot of them."

Before I could figure out how to respond to that, he walked past me to Raven, stopped in front of her, and said, "There you are, love. I've been waiting for you."

Raven glanced at him in surprise. His grin got even wider, and he pulled her onto the dance floor.

I recognized a familiar presence behind me. Sky. There was nothing sloppy about Sky's being or her power. Everything about her was clear, precise, and honed, like an elegant arrow.

"So, what do you think of this place?" Sky asked.

"It's . . . intense."

She looked at me and laughed. "That's a good word for it. There are more blood witches here than you may ever see in one place again. Some of them highly eccentric."

"What do you mean?" I asked. Sky knew so much about the world I'd only recently come to be part of.

She nodded toward a woman spinning in place to the beat, one arm stretched high overhead. "That one, for instance. She'll only cast spells that involve using nightshade. And he," she said, gesturing toward a small, dark-haired man at the bar, "spent years living in a cave on the coast of Scotland."

"Why?"

"Teaching himself to work with the sea. He's remarkable at scrying with water. And he has a strong affinity for the ocean and its creatures."

"Sky, *ma chère*." A tall, elegant woman in a silver gown came up, kissed Sky on both cheeks, and began a rapid exchange in French.

I watched, slightly awed.

"That's Mathilde," Sky said as the Frenchwoman moved on. "Sorry I didn't introduce you, but she was in a hurry. She's got an amazing greenhouse on her roof. Every herb a witch could want."

"How do you know all these people?" I asked.

"Some I know from Europe. Others I met coming here with Hunter," she explained. "This is a good place for him to make connections."

I glanced around but didn't see Hunter's blond hair anywhere.

Sky answered my unasked question. "He's upstairs, talking to some people. Trying to get leads."

A shout drew our attention back to the dance floor, where a space had opened around Raven and her partner. They were doing some kind of dance that involved a lot of athletic gyrating and shimmying.

I glanced at Sky. Her face was blank, neutral, but her eyes never left Raven and her partner. As if conscious of her gaze, the wild guy looked straight at her and laughed.

I felt sudden sympathy for Sky. "Don't let them upset you." As the words left my mouth, I was shocked at my own presumptuousness. Me, consoling Sky?

But she simply gave me a rueful half smile. "I'll get over it. Raven has to be who she is."

She nodded toward Robbie and the gorgeous girl dancing with him. Robbie looked mystified by the attention.

"He still doesn't understand how attractive he is," Sky said. "I wonder if Bree does."

Bree was still standing in the café, three men around her, but her gaze was focused across the floor on Robbie.

"Maybe she's starting to," I said.

Hunter came up behind me then, and I felt a thrill along my nerve endings as he rested his hands lightly on my hips. "How are you doing?" he asked.

"I'm a little overwhelmed," I answered, turning to face him.

He gave me an apologetic smile. "I should have prepared you."

"No, it's okay. Sky's orienting me. It's . . . fascinating. I just didn't expect it."

"Yes, well, meet your people," he said wryly.

"Did you talk to the DJ?" Sky wanted to know.

Hunter nodded. "If he knows anything, he's not telling. But I did find someone who used to date a member of Amyranth. He'll talk to me, but not here. I've arranged to meet him tomorrow at a ridiculous hour of the morning, at the most inconvenient, out-of-the-way place he could think of." He gave Sky a grin. "Sorry. I know you're not a morning person. But I really need you with me. This one sounds like he might give me some trouble."

Sky nodded. "Fine. Just promise you'll buy me a coffee."

My rational, mathematical self told me I was being silly—Hunter was keeping me out for my own safety—but I couldn't help feeling irked at the way they both just took it for granted that Sky was the one who helped Hunter, that the two of them were a team, while I was just a bumbling novice who had to be kept out of harm's way. It wasn't fair—especially not now. It was *my* dream that had started this, after all.

A black light flared above us, turning Hunter's white shirt neon purple, his hair a bright silky lavender. He kissed me lightly on the mouth. "I've got to go now, but I'll be back. Dance, why don't you?"

"Oh, thank you very much," I muttered. "You know how much I love dancing. Especially alone."

But he was already moving past me to have a quick whispered conference with Sky, which did nothing to improve my mood. Then he headed off toward the stage. The tall African American man pointed at Hunter with a knowing grin, then made his way down from the stage to talk to him. I had to admit, it was impressive seeing how at ease Hunter was with so many people. I knew I could never extract information from strangers like that.

Sky drifted back toward me, and I had the feeling that Hunter had told her to look out for me. My irritation deepened. Luckily I was relieved of the need to make awkward conversation by Robbie, who came up to us looking sweaty and exhausted. "Man, that girl can move," he said, waving at his partner. He blinked in surprise as a waitress approached him with a glass of wine balanced on a round tray.

"The lady over there"—she indicated a tall woman with long, ebony hair who was dressed entirely in leather—"sends it to you with her compliments."

"Uh, tell her thanks, would you?" Robbie sounded flustered. "But I don't drink."

"I'll tell her," the waitress said reluctantly. "But if you don't want to offend her—and I'd advise you not to—you won't send the wine back."

Robbie smiled weakly at the woman in leather and took the glass of wine.

I gave a low whistle. "You're getting a lot of attention tonight." I peeked covertly at Bree and was glad to see that she hadn't missed the exchange with Leather Woman, either.

She'd stopped even pretending to flirt with the guys around her and was just standing there, looking sulky.

Robbie, however, didn't look pleased. "It's a little freaky. Two witches have asked me out tonight."

"You have something against us?" I teased him.

"Not you," he said seriously. "But apart from the fact that I'm in love with Bree, I want a relationship of equals, not someone who can put spells on me without my even knowing."

I winced. When I was just getting acquainted with Wicca, I'd given Robbie a spelled potion to help heal his acne, which had been really out of control. It had done the job—in fact, it had more than done the job; it had gone so far as to correct his terrible eyesight—but Robbie had been upset with me for doing magick on him without telling him.

"What is his problem?" Sky said suddenly. Her eyes were on Raven and the long-haired guy. "Is he a complete exhibitionist?"

I looked, too. The guy had taken off his shirt. His body was thin but looked hard and well muscled.

Raven sent an amused glance toward Sky, as if to say, Do you believe this? Her dancing partner put his hands on her butt and pulled her close, and then pinwheels of colored light were raining down around them, and Raven was laughing, trying to catch one in her hand. The guy traced a sign in the air, and three of them rested on her palm.

I couldn't suppress a gasp. I was half appalled at his recklessness, half delighted by his clever, beautiful magick.

"Oh, man," Robbie muttered. "What is that?"

"It's showy and irresponsible, that's what it is," Sky said, sounding angry. "That cocky little bugger. Anyone could be watching him."

Raven and the guy were dancing close now, grinding pelvises. "That's enough," Sky said, and strode toward them. I saw her take Raven's arm and say something in her ear.

"Maybe I'd better go find Bree," Robbie said with a sigh. "If she hasn't already left with someone else."

"She wouldn't do that," I told him.

"You don't think so?" Robbie's smile was sad as he moved away. It made me want to shake Bree. She really liked Robbie. Why couldn't she just let things happen with him?

I headed for the café and got a Diet Coke. Then I looked around for Hunter. Nowhere in sight. I sighed, too, and tried not to feel too much like a wallflower.

A woman in a short black dress sauntered up to me. "Don't be so self-conscious, *chica*," she said. She was beautiful, with coffee-colored skin and black hair that framed her face in waves. "All this energy spent thinking you are not beautiful enough, not good enough. It's a waste. You must take all this healing energy you have and make a salve for your own heart, no? Life is too short to be so hard on yourself."

I stood there, blinking stupidly. She was gazing into my eyes, into my soul, and I felt stripped, vulnerable.

"Um . . . excuse me," I said. "I have to go."

I shut down my senses and bolted for a door marked Exit. I didn't plan to go far. I just needed to be out of there, away from all that magick for a few minutes.

I thought the door would lead to the street. Instead I found myself in a small courtyard planted with skinny oak saplings. I wasn't alone. A man with short-cropped, silver-flecked dark hair stood in the yard, staring up at a big square of the night sky. Even with my senses shut down I felt a surge of energy—deep, vital energy, not the fractured, hectic kind that ruled inside. Whether it was from the man or the giant orange moon, I couldn't be sure.

I sat down on a bench at the edge of the courtyard and gazed up at the moon, wondering what he was seeing. As I looked, I felt my frazzled nerve endings begin to relax. The moon was so eternal, so familiar in this place where everything else was so strange. I breathed deeply, and peace began to creep back into my body.

"The moon is our anchor," the man said without looking at me.

Ordinarily I would have been startled by these bizarre words coming from a total stranger. But at that moment my only thought was, Yes. I didn't feel the need to respond aloud, and he didn't seem to expect me to.

I stared at the moon, letting it anchor me.

4

Glamor

July 15, 1981

I write this on the ferry crossing the Irish Sea. I'm part of a delegation from Liathach, bound for western Ireland, to the very village where I was born, Ballynigel. We're going, as clansmen, to pay a visit to the Belwicket coven. I don't remember any of them at all. I'm very curious to see a Woodbane coven that forswore evil more than a hundred years ago. Bright magick and dark, the Woodbanes have never feared either. How Belwicket could have given up fully half of our ancient, essential powers, I can't fathom. But that is what we're going to observe. And we'll see whether there is anything in Ballynigel strong enough to resist us. We can't—won't—risk opposition. If we find it . . . there has been talk of the dark wave.

Mother stands near the bow with Greer, probably gossiping about the bairns. The two grannies are both mad for little Iona, and a sweet thing she is, though every bit as much trouble as her brother, Kyle. I take it as a good sign that Greer invited me to be part of this mission. Finally she is admitting me to Liathach's inner circle of leaders.

Grania, of course, didn't want me to go. "You can't leave me with two little ones to care for all on my own," she kept telling me. But I can and I have. The dream is still with me, and I long to see Ballynigel again.

—Neimhidh

I gazed up at the winter moon. I could feel my own power coursing through me, untainted by questions of whether I'd misused it or whether I was worth the sacrifice of Cal's life. It was as if my world had silently, subtly slipped into perfect balance. A few yards away from me the dark-haired man stood silent. He hadn't looked at me once, but I felt a strange connection between us, as sure and strong as if he'd thrown me a rope.

Where are you? Hunter's witch message almost made me jump. Reluctantly I stood up. The man nodded, as if acknowledging that I was leaving, but didn't say a word. I returned to the club, feeling I'd just been given a strange but lovely gift.

I found my friends gathered on a semicircular leather couch in the bar area. The showy witch Raven had been dancing with sat next to her on the very end of the couch.

Sky looked up as I approached. "Morgan, this is Killian," she said, her voice perfectly neutral, which made me wonder what I'd missed.

Killian gave me a grin, held out his hand, and said, "Enchanted."

Hunter made room for me beside him. Killian's dark eyes flickered between us, and I wondered if he could tell that just sitting next to Hunter made my whole body feel more alive.

Bree was looking at Killian with a calculating expression. "So you're another Brit?" she asked.

"Yeah, we're all over New York, a ruddy plague of us," he admitted cheerfully.

His accent was different from Hunter's and Sky's. I was glad when Robbie asked, "Which part of England?"

"Oh, I've done the whole miserable U.K. Born in Scotland, went to school in London, spent time in Ireland, summers in Wales and the Shetlands. And in all those places it rains too bleeding much. I'm still damp." He held out his arm to me. "Can you see the moss?"

I couldn't help laughing, liking him. He was definitely appealing. His features weren't perfect, like Cal's had been, and he didn't have Hunter's classic, chiseled bone structure, but he had energy. There was something wild, almost animal, about him. I wondered which clan he belonged to. But I knew I couldn't ask. Among witches, that question was considered very intrusive.

Killian got to his feet. "I'm going to get a beer. Anyone want one?"

"You're twenty-one?" I asked, surprised. He didn't look any older than the rest of us.

"Almost twenty," he admitted with a grin, "but I age well."

As he spoke, he drew a sign in the air, and the planes of his face became softer and fuller. Lines appeared across his forehead, and a crease deepened between his brows. Anyone would have thought he was pushing thirty. "Now . . . beer, wine, scotch, anyone?"

"I'll have a beer, too," Raven said, looking smitten.

"A Sprite would be great," Robbie said.

"Sprite it is," Killian said graciously, but I could sense mockery.

"He's good," Bree said as Killian started off for the crowded bar.

"It was just a glamor," Sky said dismissively. "A trick of the eye."

Bree looked at me. "What do you think of him?"

I shrugged, unsure of how to answer. On one level, I couldn't help liking him, his cheerful irreverence and the fact that he seemed to be having such a good time just being Killian. But there was also something about him that alarmed me, something dangerous in his raw, animal spirits. And there was the fact that when he cast that glamor, I felt pure envy. I knew I had the power to pull off magick like that, yet my lack of experience held me back. Alyce didn't know how to cast glamors, and neither did I.

Hunter gave me an odd look. "What's bothering you?"

"I don't know." I shifted in my seat, annoyed with myself for being so competitive. A good Wiccan would be able to simply enjoy Killian's power for what it was.

"I'm not sure I trust him," Hunter said thoughtfully. His eyes followed Killian as he scored the two beers and Robbie's soda.

Raven lit a cigarette and blew smoke through her nostrils at us. "What is your collective problem?" she asked. "So Killian shows off a little with his magick. All it means is he's different."

"That's one word for it," said Sky, her voice acid-edged.

Killian returned then, his glamor dissolved, and gave Robbie and Raven their drinks. "How long are you going to be in the city?" he asked Raven.

Raven started to answer, only to be silenced by a warning look from Hunter. "Uh, I'm not sure," she said.

"So, will I see you again?" he persisted.

"Maybe," she said. She slid a quick glance at Sky, as if to ask, How far will you let me push you? before she added, "Why don't you give me your number?"

He gave her a wide-eyed look. "Would you believe I'm staying with friends and I can't remember their number? How about you give me your number?"

It was a transparent lie, and I wondered why he told it, especially since he didn't make any real effort to be convincing. I could feel Sky reaching a silent boil. Raven must have felt it, too, because she shrugged, downed her beer, and got to her feet. "Same here," she said. "Can't remember it. Guess I'll see you when I see you."

Killian held out his hand and pulled her to him. Then he gave her a quick kiss, teetering on the edge between friendly and sexual.

I glanced at Sky in alarm. Her face was set, her nostrils flared.

"Raven, we're leaving now," Hunter said loudly.

Raven looked at Killian and shrugged. "Gotta go."

Killian's dark brows rose. "Must you?"

"Yes, we must," Hunter said. We retrieved our coats and trailed out of the club into the frigid streets.

We started back to the apartment. Sky and Raven walked ahead, maintaining an icy distance between themselves and us. Robbie slung an arm around Bree's shoulders, and they walked on like that, quiet and compatible. Whatever ups and downs they'd had during the evening, they seemed to have ended it on an upward trend.

Hunter was quiet, too, and walking slowly enough that we fell behind Robbie and Bree after a block or two. "Thinking about your job?" I guessed.

He nodded in a distracted way.

How could he focus so intensely on something so nebulous, so unformed? I couldn't—especially not when I was around him. I felt the familiar rush of insecurity. Did he even love me? He'd never said he did.

Of course he does, I told myself. He's just not as obvious about it as Cal was.

Feeling suddenly sad, I pulled my jacket tighter. Above us white stars blazed through a clear black night. The moon was gone, dropped somewhere behind the Manhattan skyline.

"Cold?" Hunter asked, pulling me against him.

"I'm not so sure I want to go to that club again," I told him. "The amount of magick flying around was almost too much."

"It was intense, that's true. But it's good to be exposed to lots of magick, coming from lots of sources. Besides just increasing your general knowledge, it will help you to recognize and deal with dark magick. Which, as you know, is especially important for you."

I felt my chest tighten. We'd already talked about this

more than once—about the fact that Selene had been part of a larger conspiracy, that her death probably didn't mean I was safe from other members of her coven or from other factions altogether. I'm going to be looking over my shoulder for the rest of my life, I thought bleakly.

Hunter pulled me to a stop under a streetlight. It cast harsh shadows on the planes of his face, making his cheekbones look razor sharp. "Don't worry," he said gently. "I'm looking after you. And you can look after yourself pretty well, too, you know. Besides, if Amyranth knows about you at all, they'll know you're high on the council's radar right now."

I thought of Killian. "Maybe I need to learn the art of magickal disguise."

"That's the least of it." Hunter frowned at me. "Why are you so eager to be casting glamors, anyway? I could see it in your eyes tonight. They went round with envy when Killian did his little parlor trick."

"It's not just envy," I said, thinking it through aloud. "It's knowing that I have the power to be like those other witches, except I don't know how to use it. It's like being given the key to this fabulous palace and seeing all these gorgeous rooms lit up inside but not knowing how to get the key into the lock."

"Is that bad?" he asked. "You've only been practicing magick for two and a half months. And learning to wield magick properly is a lifetime's work."

Oh Goddess, how sick I was of hearing that! I started walking again.

Hunter reached out, caught my arm, and pulled me toward him. "Morgan. You know that I want you to be able to put that key in the lock, don't you? I'm not trying to keep you out of the palace. I want you to come fully into your power, to be able to use every bit of magick in you." His fingertips stroked my face, and I felt myself moving toward him. "I just don't want you or anyone else getting hurt in the process."

"I know," I breathed as he gently lowered his head to mine. Then his arms wrapped around me and our mouths met and I felt all the tension of the evening melt away. I opened myself to Hunter, and it was like a river of sapphire light poured into me, like he was washing me in his magick and his love. I felt my own heart open and my power moving, streaming through my body, twining with his. It felt like that spot on the Manhattan sidewalk was the center of the universe and the night and all its stars spun out from us. In that moment, in that place, I had no doubts, no insecurities.

Love, I thought. The ultimate magick.

Hunter and I were the last ones to get back to the apartment. Inside we found Robbie in the kitchen, emptying a bag of popcorn into a bowl, Bree taking sheets and blankets from the linen closet, and Sky and Raven standing at opposite ends of the living room. Mr. Warren was nowhere in sight.

Robbie consulted his watch as I hung up my jacket. "Where have you two been?" he asked, sounding like a disapproving parent.

"We . . . got a little lost," Hunter said, flashing me a quick, secret smile that made my cold cheeks turn a shade more pink.

Raven grabbed a handful of popcorn. "So, where's everyone sleeping?" she asked.

No one answered. Sky stared out the window, Robbie concentrated on the popcorn, and Bree murmured something about pillowcases and returned to the linen closet.

Hunter's green eyes locked on me, and I found myself looking away, unaccountably shy all over again. Was it possible that we'd actually wind up in the same bed? Even if we did, I was fairly sure no one was going to be doing much fooling around—the apartment was just too cramped. I was secretly relieved. I wasn't quite ready for that. But my heart was pounding at the thought of sleeping with some part of my body touching Hunter's. I longed to be with him for a few peaceful hours without the confusion of consciousness. I longed to wake up in his arms.

I wondered what Bree and Robbie wanted to do. They seemed to be getting along now, but I wasn't about to discount what Bree had said in the market.

Bree, holding an armful of linens, cleared her throat. "Well, the living room couch folds out to a double bed. The bed in the guest room is a trundle bed, so it has another mattress under it, and there's a couch in the study." She flashed an overly bright smile that proved she felt every bit as nervous as I did.

Raven made an impatient noise. "Let's get it over with already. How do you want to split it up?"

Again no one answered. Finally Hunter spoke up. "The way I see it, Mr. Warren's being kind enough to host us. Whatever we do shouldn't upset him."

Bree's eyes lingered on Robbie with a mix of desire and regret. "I'm not sure my dad would notice if we mixed it up," she admitted, "but it's probably a good idea not to find out.

Better to keep the girls and guys separate."

I tried not to look disappointed and told myself that Bree and Hunter were right.

"Robbie and I can take the study," Hunter volunteered.

Robbie walked over to the pile of luggage in the living room and picked up his pack and a small green stuff sack. "Air mattress," he explained.

"Morgan and I can take the guest room," Bree said. "That's the room I usually sleep in when I come down here, anyway."

"Sounds good," I said, surprised and pleased that Bree had chosen me for her roommate.

"That means Sky and I have the living room," Raven said.

Sky said, "I think I'll go out for a walk. Don't wait up for me."

Raven stared at her in disbelief. "Oh, come on! I can't believe you're still upset. I was just flirting with him. It was harmless."

"That's not how I saw it," Sky said, her voice tight.

Raven made a face. "Oh, Jesus."

"Look, we'll just rearrange," Hunter said, sounding weary. "Robbie and I can share the foldout in the living room. Sky can have the study."

"And where does that leave me?" Raven demanded, one hand on her hip.

Bree took the air mattress from Robbie. "You can sleep in the guest room with me and Morgan," she said. "Really, it will be totally comfortable."

"Brilliant," said Hunter. "Then everybody's happy."

I don't think anyone actually believed that, but we all went off to our agreed-upon quarters.

For the next fifteen minutes Bree and Raven and I

worked on inflating the air mattress and getting sheets and blankets on all three beds. I was fighting a sense of crashing disappointment. How did my romantic getaway with Hunter turn into a sleepover with the girls?

Bree grabbed a robe from behind the door and announced she was going to take a shower, leaving me in the guest room with Raven. I pulled my nightgown out of my pack. It was a simple white cotton gown cut straight across the chest with skinny ribbon shoulder straps. Actually, it was Mary K.'s; she had loaned it to me. I didn't even own a nightgown.

"You want to wear this," Mary K. had assured me. "Trust me, Hunter will love it."

Hunter's not even going to see it, I thought grumpily.

Raven had changed into a loose black T-shirt with the neck and arms cut out. She was sitting on the air mattress, examining the black polish on her toenails. "Sky can be a cold bitch sometimes," she muttered.

"Maybe," I agreed. "But I think your flirting with Killian was hard on her."

Raven snorted. "She knows that didn't mean anything."

"Then why was she so freaked?"

"I don't know," Raven said irritably.

I wondered how far into this conversation I should go. Though we were in the same coven, Raven and I had never exactly been friends. She was a senior and hung out with a much tougher crowd than I ever had. The idea of me, who'd been kissed by all of two boys, giving Raven Meltzer romantic advice was a joke.

I was brushing out my hair when Raven said, "So tell me—

what's your theory? On Sky, I mean."

Okay, it was definitely a weird night. I chose my words carefully. "Sky cares about you, and you hurt her. I think her coldness is the way she reacts to being hurt. If I were you, I'd give her another chance," I said. Then, before things could get any weirder, I grabbed my toothbrush and headed for the bathroom.

Robbie was already standing in line, listening to the sound of the shower. I wondered if that meant Hunter was alone in the living room but didn't have the nerve to ask.

"Bree's still in there," Robbie reported, rolling his eyes at the bathroom door. "I think she's washing every strand of hair on her head individually."

"That's okay—I'll wait." A daring idea suddenly occurred to me. "Robbie . . . how would you feel about switching places with me a little later tonight?"

Robbie's eyebrows rose. "Morganita, you sly dog!"

"Not for the whole night or anything. Maybe for an hour or so."

"I dunno," Robbie said. "That means you get an hour with Hunter, and I've got that same hour with Bree and Raven."

"We'll wait till one," I said. "Everyone should be asleep. You can just slip in next to Bree. Raven will never know."

Robbie eyed me doubtfully. "What if Raven wakes up?"

"Then just explain you were sleepwalking and stumbled into the wrong room."

"Yeah, that's believable."

"Oh, come on, Robbie. Please."

"Shhh," he whispered. "Okay, I'll do it."

My heart skipped a beat as Hunter walked toward us,

toothbrush in hand. He was wearing a long-sleeved black T-shirt over gray sweats that just seemed to emphasize how long and lean he was.

I felt his eyes on me, taking in the white nightgown and my hair brushed out and hanging loose, and I knew that Mary K. had been right. I could feel Hunter's senses reaching out to me, wanting me, drawing me toward him.

Robbie must have sensed the electricity between us. "I'm going to hang in the kitchen," he said. "But if Bree ever gets out of the bathroom, I'm first."

Neither Hunter nor I said anything until he left. Then Hunter came close. "You look beautiful," he said in a husky voice.

"Thanks. Um—you too," I said in my eloquent way. My hands, ridiculously, trembled a little, and I folded my arms so he wouldn't notice. I debated whether or not to tell him what Robbie and I had been planning. But before I'd worked up my nerve, he spoke in a rush.

"Do you think I could possibly persuade you to change places with Robbie for a little while tonight?" he asked. I heard the anxiety in his voice, the fear that I might say no, and I loved him so, so much.

"I already asked him," I said, my heart hammering.

Hunter blew out his breath and grinned. His eyes danced with emerald green light. "Great minds . . ." he said, and bent to kiss me. Just then the bathroom door swung open and a cloud of steam floated out.

"Whoops," Bree said.

Hunter and I pulled apart. "Robbie," I called, grateful for the steam that hid my red cheeks. "The bathroom's yours."

An hour later we were all tucked in. I was too excited to even consider sleep. Periodically I extended my senses, identifying the patterns of the people in the apartment. Bree was sleeping, and so were Raven and Sky. Hunter and Robbie were both wide awake.

Finally it was one A.M. Moving quietly so as not to wake Bree and Raven, I made my way out of the guest room. In the living room a single candle flickered. Hunter and Robbie were sitting on opposite ends of the couch, waiting for me.

"Bree," Robbie whispered. "Is she—"

"Asleep," I told him. "Be careful you don't startle her. Any sign of Mr. Warren?"

Hunter shook his head. "Not yet."

I was keenly aware of his being just a few feet from me. My heart began to beat faster, and that funny anticipation feeling—that mix of pleasure with just a thread of uncertainty—began to hum through me. I waited till Robbie had gone, and then I sat beside Hunter.

"I was afraid you wouldn't come," he said. He reached out and closed one hand over mine. "I thought you might fall asleep."

"Almost did," I teased.

"Did you really?" he asked.

"No," I admitted, suddenly feeling vulnerable and unsure. It occurred to me again that Hunter had never told me he loved me, though I'd told him I loved him. Was it just a guy thing, not being able to say the words? Or did he not feel the same way? Hunter was honest to a fault, and I was certain that he cared about me. But maybe it wasn't love, and that's why he'd never said the words. Could Bree be right about love? Maybe Hunter was about to break my heart and hand it back to me in little pieces.

Maybe I shouldn't be here now, I thought, feeling a tickle of panic. Maybe I should just go back to my own bed, not get close to anything I can't handle.

Then Hunter turned over my hand and began to gently stroke the underside of my arm. His touch sent shivers of delight racing through me.

"You were like a vision, you know," he said, his voice soft and low. "Standing there in the hall in that innocent gown, your hair shining, holding a toothbrush of all things. I just wanted to run away with you."

"Really?" I whispered. "Where to?"

"I don't know. Didn't think it through that far." He brushed back a strand of hair from my face. "You know, I never had second thoughts about becoming a Seeker. It seemed necessary, fated. But lately . . ." His voice trailed off on a note of longing.

"Lately what?"

"I wish there were a way to take a break from it. I wish I could just steal away with you for a while."

My heart was pounding like a drum. I fought desperately to keep things grounded, realistic. "My parents probably wouldn't be too keen on that idea," I said.

"Right. Parents," he said. "They probably wouldn't approve of this, either." He bent forward and kissed the side of my neck.

Chills raced through me. The energy flowing between us felt so strong and right and good. I didn't want to walk away from it. Not anymore. Gently I lifted his head so that I could put my mouth on his. He wrapped his arms around me.

At first our kisses were soft, searching, as if we were just getting to know each other. Hunter's hands slid along my nightgown, caressing my waist, my side. Every inch of my body was alight with desire. Everything in me streamed toward Hunter. I slid my hand under his shirt, felt the smooth skin of his chest over a hard sheath of muscle. Gently he pushed me backward so we were lying on the foldout bed. He pulled back for a moment, and I saw his face in the light from the window, intent as always. But now, this time, he was totally focused on *me*. His lips came down on mine again, harder now, more urgent.

Then, without warning, Hunter broke away.

"What's wrong?" I asked, breathless.

"Don't you sense him?"

And then I did. It was Mr. Warren, coming down the hall.

"He can't!" I groaned. "It's not fair."

"But he is." Hunter held me close with one arm. He ran his other hand along my face and kissed me gently. "We'd better call it a night."

"No! Can't we do a spell to make him think he's dropped his keys and has to go back down to the garage, or—"

Hunter swatted at me lightly. "You know better. Come on, now. Go give Bree and Robbie some warning."

I got up with a groan. I could hear Mr. Warren's footsteps coming down the hallway. "Okay." I leaned forward and gave Hunter one last kiss. "To be continued," I promised.

5

Gifts of the Mage

July 16, 1981

We've been in Ballynigel less than twenty-four hours, and everything has changed. I know now why I kept dreaming of this place, why I've felt drawn back here, as though there were an invisible string connecting it to my heart.

I first saw Maeve Riordan yesterday. She was not among those who welcomed our boat. She was off gathering moss for a poultice and didn't come back into the village until we were in a meeting with Belwicket's elders. We were in the house of Mackenna, their high priestess, beginning to ask those questions whose answers would determine Belwicket's fate, though they didn't realize it, poor sods. And in walks Mackenna's daughter, a girl of nineteen with a mud-streaked skirt and a basket overflowing with drippy moss.

I had the strangest sensation that I'd waited twenty-two years to see her. It was as though my life were slightly unreal until that moment. She seemed fey—a luminous creature—and at the same time utterly familiar, as if I'd known and loved her my whole life.

Everything about Maeve enchants me. The light that dances in her eyes, the rhythm of her speech, the sound of her laughter, the grace of her hands, and, of course, the magick that sparkles around her. She has a great deal of raw power—as much as Selene, I think. Selene was a different package, though. She'd been honing her magick for years, had studied, sacrificed, undergone a Great Trial, even. In Maeve it's simply a matter of her birthright. She takes it for granted, doesn't yet realize how much power courses through her.

Of course, there is the matter of Belwicket having forsworn the old Woodbane ways. Still, I'm certain we'll get past that. She feels the same way about me that I do about her—I can see it in her eyes. I will show Maeve how to realize her true power. I'll convince her that my way is the right one.

So this is what love feels like, the love that lasts for all time. When it happens, there are no questions, no doubts. I know that now. And I know the dress on the line . . . it can only have been hers.

—Neimhidh

Friday morning, I woke to unfamiliar sounds filtering through the guest room door—Mr. Warren making coffee while having a heated phone conversation about depositions.

On the mattress next to me Bree stretched and opened her eyes. "Sleep well?" she asked with a drowsy smile.

I blushed. "Yeah. How about you?"

She shrugged. "Fine," she said in a neutral voice.

Raven's eyes shot open, ringed with black eye makeup she hadn't washed off. "What time is it?" she demanded.

"Just after nine-thirty," Bree answered. "We should get moving. I want to go to Diva's this morning. It's in SoHo. You guys should come, too—they've got great clothes, and they're really cheap."

I could feel that Hunter and Sky weren't in the apartment; they must have already left for their meeting with the mysterious contact Hunter had met last night. "Uh—okay," I agreed. Maybe I could find an outfit that was slightly more appropriate for the city.

Raven shook her head. "I'll pass. Not my kind of place," she said.

"Okay." Bree got up, took her robe from its hook, and went out into the kitchen.

Raven rubbed her temples. "I feel like hell. I need a shower," she said, and padded off to the bathroom.

I got dressed, my thoughts on Hunter and how good it had felt to be with him last night, how I wished it could have lasted longer.

I quickly plaited my hair into a braid and glanced in the mirror on the closet door. In a black turtleneck and jeans, I was presentable. I went out into the living room, where I found Robbie folding up the sofa bed. He was dressed in jeans and a blue plaid flannel shirt, and his hair was still mussed from sleep.

"Morning," Robbie said. "Hunter left a note for you." He pulled a folded piece of paper from his pocket and handed it to me.

> Morgan—
>   I'll meet you back at the apartment by 10:30.
>   —Hunter

Of course, the thing that I noticed was that he'd signed it Hunter. Not: Love, Hunter or even Yours, Hunter. Just plain Hunter. Very romantic.

Mr. Warren rushed out of the apartment, briefcase in hand, and Bree came into the living room. "What's up?"

I showed her Hunter's note. Bree made a face. "I wanted to go the coffee shop downstairs and get some breakfast. But I guess we'll wait."

So we waited. Raven emerged from the guest room in yet another skintight black outfit. She seemed a little annoyed that Sky was still out. Bree and Robbie weren't talking, I noticed, and Robbie was doing his best to pretend he was okay about it. He headed out, saying a little too casually that he wanted to do some exploring on his own. First, though, we agreed that we'd all meet up for lunch at a deli on the Upper West Side at two that afternoon.

Ten-thirty came and went. By eleven Hunter and Sky still hadn't come back, and Bree and I were dying to get out, get food, do something besides sit around the apartment. And I was getting worried.

Finally I sent Hunter a witch message. But after ten minutes he hadn't responded. My pulse rate picked up a little. Was he okay?

"Well?" Raven asked.

"Nothing," I said, trying to keep my voice calmer than I felt.

"That boy has really got to join the twenty-first century and get a cell phone," Bree said.

I sent another, more emphatic witch message to Hunter, trying to determine if he was okay.

After a moment I got a response from Sky: We're fine. That was it. Hunter didn't bother to reply at all. Again I couldn't help a surge of irritation. Maybe I wasn't being rational about this, but it sure felt like I was being shut out.

"I just heard from Sky," I told the others. "They're okay. But I don't think they're going to be back for a while."

"Then let's shop," Bree said.

Raven yawned. "I'm going back to bed," she announced. "I am not a morning person."

Half an hour and two pastries later, Bree and I stood on the cast-iron steps of Diva's on West Broadway. I'd been there once before, but even if you lived in Widow's Vale and had never been to the city, you knew about Diva's. It was a mecca for the young and broke.

Bree led the way inside the huge warehouse of a store. Rap blared from the speakers. There were stacks of T-shirts in every color of the rainbow; pants in reds and blues and petal pinks; sweatshirts in olive green, neon yellow, and baby blue.

Bree started poking through the vintage racks and found a man's long-sleeved black shirt with gray pearl buttons. "Maybe I should buy this for Robbie," she mused. Unlike the rest of us, Bree had a generous allowance.

I couldn't keep my mouth shut. "Bree, do you or do you not like that boy?"

She looked at me, startled. "I told you. I'm completely crazy about him."

"Well, then please stop treating him like crap!" I said. "It's painful to watch."

Bree put the shirt back and calmly moved on to a rack of trendier clothing. "If you want to know the truth," she said, "it's Robbie who should be treating me better."

"What?" I stared at her.

"At the club last night," she said. "He danced and flirted with all those women."

"Three, and they all came on to him," I argued.

"Don't blame them. It's Robbie's responsibility to say no," said Bree. "If he really wants to be with me, why did he encourage them?"

"Maybe because he wasn't getting any encouragement from you?" I suggested. "Come on, Bree. You had your own little entourage over by the café. What kind of message did that send? Besides, you know none of those women mattered. Robbie doesn't care about anyone except you. Can't you see that?"

Bree held up a slinky black cocktail dress. "I know Robbie's trying," she acknowledged. "But so am I." She frowned, put the dress back, and moved on to a rack of pants. "This is just the way relationships go."

"Only because you steer them that way."

Bree sighed. "I don't want to talk about this right now. I'm hitting the dressing room. Are you going to try anything on?"

"I'll meet you in there," I told her. Obviously the conversation was over.

I quickly scooped up a couple of V-necked T-shirts and a few camisoles. Camisoles were my official choice for underwear.

Having nothing to put in the cups, I'd given up on bras.

There was a line for the dressing rooms, so I shouted for Bree. She yelled back that I should share her room.

I found Bree wearing a stretchy bronze-colored top with black knit hip-hugger pants. She looked amazing. "Think Robbie will like this?" she asked.

I groaned and slid down onto the floor of the tiny cubicle. I decided to try one more time. "Listen, I know for a fact that Robbie loves you. And you obviously care about him. Why can't you trust that and stop trying to undermine all the good stuff? Why can't you just let yourself love him and be happy?"

Bree rolled her eyes. "Because," she said with absolute certainty, "in real life things just don't work that way, Morgan."

Didn't they? I wondered. I thought again about Bree's mom walking out on her and her dad. That had to be the root of all her warped ideas about love.

Or did Bree really know something I didn't?

Twenty minutes later Bree and I left Diva's, each of us carrying a neon pink shopping bag. Bree had bought the bronze-top outfit, a chartreuse day pack, and a black T-shirt for Robbie. I'd gotten a cobalt blue tee and a lilac camisole, which pretty much shot my clothing budget.

"What's next?" I asked, cheered by our retail therapy.

Bree looked thoughtful. "There's a fabulous shoe store right around the corner, and there's a shop close by that specializes in African jewelry. There's also an aromatherapy place off Wooster," she added.

"Let's check that out."

We hadn't gone more than a block when my witch senses

began to tug at me. "Bree, can we go this way?" I asked, pointing down Broome Street.

She shrugged good-naturedly. "Why not?"

I followed my senses the way a spider follows its own silken thread and found myself in an alley off Broome Street. Hanging over a narrow doorway at the end of the alley was a square white banner with a green wheel printed on it. In the center of the green wheel was a purple pentagram.

"The Wheel of the Year," Bree said. "The diagram for the eight Wiccan sabbats."

The feel of magick grew stronger with every step we took. When we reached the shop, a sign on the black cast-iron door made me smile: Gifts of the Mage: Specializing in Books of Magick and the Occult. And beneath it in smaller letters: Welcome, Friends.

I pushed open the door, causing a brass bell to ring, and stepped into a cool, dim, high-ceilinged space. I didn't see the sort of general Wiccan supplies that Practical Magick stocked, but a wall of cabinets behind the counter held essential oils in bottles that looked positively ancient. A deep balcony ran around the walls halfway up, with more bookshelves and shabby armchairs in alcoves.

Bree walked toward mahogany shelves stacked with tarot decks. "Oh, they have a reproduction of that gorgeous Italian deck I saw in the Pierpont Morgan Library," she said.

My witch senses were still prickling. Was there something here that I was meant to find? I glanced up at the black metal staircase that led to the balcony floor.

"Alyce recommended a book on scrying," I told Bree, "but she didn't have it in stock. Maybe I can find it here."

Already absorbed in tarot decks, Bree mumbled an okay.

Following the store directory, I climbed the stairs to the balcony and began to search for the divination section. The scent of old leather tickled my nose. I could almost feel centuries of spells whispering to me. *Find me, invoke me. I'm yours, I'm made for your power.* I passed sections labeled Oracles and Emanations, Amulets and Talismans. It felt good be among so many books filled with so much knowledge.

I rounded the end of the aisle and came face-to-face with a large section labeled Divination. Just beyond it, at the end of this next aisle, I saw a man seated in an armchair next to a potted tree of some sort. I stopped, confused by the feeling of familiarity that swept over me.

Then I realized he was the same man who'd been in the courtyard of the club the night before. He was reading a book, looking as relaxed as if he were in his own living room. He wore a tweed jacket over a white shirt and faded jeans. Cropped salt-and-pepper hair softened a hawkish weathered face.

He glanced up, showing me deep-set brown eyes, and acknowledged me with a courteous nod. "We meet again," he said.

"Do you work here?" I blurted.

"No." He seemed surprised by the idea. "I teach myth and folklore at Columbia. This is just one of my more pleasant sources for reference materials." He had a faint accent, which I hadn't noticed before. Irish or Scottish, maybe—I wasn't sure. He marked his place in the book and closed it. "Was that your first time at the club, last night?" he asked.

"Yes." Sometimes I am such a brilliant conversationalist, it's really overwhelming. Why was I so tongue-tied around this man? I asked myself. It certainly wasn't a crush thing. He had to be nearly as old as my dad. And yet I felt an affinity with him, a familiarity, an attraction.

He regarded me with curiosity. "What did you think of it?"

I thought about the beautiful illusion Killian had created for Raven.

"It was a little intense, but also cool," I said. "I'd never seen witches use their magick just for pleasure."

"Personally, that's what I've always liked best about magick— using it to create beauty and pleasure in the midst of the trials life forces us to undergo."

He made a sign over the potted tree, and I watched its leaves fade, shrivel, and fall off. From the soil a green shoot grew. It was as if I were watching a movie on fast-forward. No natural plant could grow so quickly, but in the space of a minute or so a lilac bush grew against the trunk of the dead tree, and pale lilac blossoms opened, filling the air with sweet fragrance.

It was incredibly beautiful. It was also a little unnerving. It broke all the laws of nature. What would happen to the lilac? It was an outdoor plant that needed a winter's frost. It couldn't survive in a pot in a store. And I couldn't help feeling a little sorry for the healthy tree that had died for a witch's pleasure.

And what would Hunter think of this? I wondered. He'd probably consider it an irresponsible, not to mention indiscreet, use of magick. Something the council would frown on.

"The world can always use more beauty, you know," the man said, as if he'd read my doubts. "Adding beauty to the world is never irresponsible."

I didn't know how to answer. I suddenly felt very, very young and ignorant.

He seemed to sense my discomfort. "So, you came here looking for a book?"

"Yes." I was enormously relieved to remember I had a concrete reason for being there. "I'm looking for a book on scrying by Devin Dhualach."

"A good name, that," the man said. "Devin means bard, you know, so hopefully he can write. And Dhualach is an old Irish name that comes down to us from the Druids. If he's true to his ancestors, he may indeed have something useful to say about scrying."

"I—I'll just look at these shelves under divination," I said, suddenly shy and nervous.

"Good idea." The man smiled and went back to his book.

I found the Dhualach and sat down cross-legged on the floor to look through it. There were chapters on scrying with water, fire, mirrors, and *luegs*, scrying stones or crystals. There was even a macabre chapter on throwing bones, snake vertebrae being very highly recommended. There was nothing, though—at least nothing I could see on a quick skim— that dealt with how to control the visions, how to fine-tune them so I could see exactly what I needed to see.

The man from the courtyard glanced up from his book. "Not finding quite what you're looking for?" he asked.

I hesitated, aware that I had to be careful. Yet it didn't feel like he was prying. It was more that he recognized me as another blood witch and sensed my power. It wasn't the first time that had happened. David Redstone had recognized what I was the first time he saw me, even before I knew myself.

I noticed that he was looking at me oddly, as if he'd suddenly remembered something but wasn't sure whether or not he should mention it. Then he said, "You scry with fire." It was an acknowledgment rather than a question.

I nodded, and my nervousness dropped away. It was as if I'd just walked through a door into a room where we were acknowledged peers. Witch to witch. Strength to strength. Power conduit to power conduit.

"The fire shows me things, but I feel like they're often random. I don't know how to make it show me what *I'm* looking for," I admitted.

"Fire has a will of her own," he said. "Fire is ravenous, fighting control, always seeking her own pleasure. To tame her is a lifetime's work, a matter of coaxing her to reveal what you want to know. I could show you, but"—he looked at the shelves around us and smiled—"a bookstore is hardly the place to play with fire."

"That's all right," I said, trying not to sound disappointed.

The lines around his eyes crinkled. "Perhaps I can explain it through another medium. The principle's the same."

He reached into an inner pocket of his jacket and drew out a piece of clear, polished crystal, cut in the shape of a crescent moon. It wasn't big, maybe three inches across, but its surface was faceted and etched with runes and magickal symbols.

He held the crystal out to me, and I took it in my right hand. The crystal was surprisingly light, as if it belonged to a slightly altered gravity.

"I assume you know that you must ask the medium to give you a vision and that you must be specific. If what you want is to see your kitten tomorrow, specify tomorrow." I wondered how he knew I had a kitten. Then again, it wasn't uncommon for witches to have cats. "In your mind's eye picture that animal or person and send the image into the stone, asking it to accept it." His voice was soft, almost hypnotic. "The key is you must then use your power to feel the energy in the crystal—or the fire—and send its light into the future, searching for what you seek. That's really all there is to it."

"You make it sound simple," I said.

"Most things are, once they're familiar. Why don't you practice with the crystal first?" At the doubt in my eyes he said, "Hold on to the crystal if you like. I need to go downstairs and check a few books for my syllabus. Just leave the crystal by the chair when you're done with it."

I sat there debating as he went down the stairs. I didn't want to try anything complicated in the store, but maybe I could do something simple. I'd been worried about Mary K. ever since that awful night Selene kidnapped her, using her as the bait to get me. She didn't seem to remember anything about being at Selene's house—in fact, she seemed to have believed the cover story we gave my parents, which was that she had gone to the movies by herself because she was depressed. But lately she'd been having nightmares.

I'd finally learned not to underestimate anything Selene did. Rational or not, there was a part of me that worried that though Selene was dead, her magick somehow still had a hold on my sister.

Holding the crystal, I silently asked the stone to give me the vision I sought. I pictured my sister at home, sitting at the table, and asked the crystal to accept that image. I nearly dropped the stone as Mary K.'s image appeared inside it, tiny and perfect and three-dimensional. I watched her sitting at the table, then I asked the crystal to show her to me one week from now.

A stone's energy pattern is as distinct as any person's or animal's. The energy in this particular crystal was cool, glowing green-white, surging and swelling like a tide. For several breaths I let my energy ride its swells. Then I sent it surging into the future.

The image in the crescent changed. I saw Mary K. and her friend Jaycee walking out of the Widow's Vale Cineplex. The vision was so perfect and detailed, I could even see the missing X in the marquee.

Then I felt something odd, almost like a cold draft on the back of my neck. I wheeled around in alarm. Was someone watching me? Even in a place frequented by other witches, I knew it wasn't a good idea for me to work magick in public. But I could see no one else on the balcony, and when I extended my senses, I couldn't feel anyone nearby.

Focusing on the crystal again, I realized I was starting to feel tired, which was pretty common whenever I moved into a new level of magick. Knowing I wouldn't be able to maintain the spell much longer, I thanked the stone for its help and withdrew my power from it. The glowing green-white light inside it faded, and the vision of Mary K. winked out.

I'd done it. I'd called up a vision and seen exactly what I'd asked to see. This was the way magick was supposed to work.

I stood up. Then, feeling light-headed, I sat down in the chair. I was vaguely aware that Bree must be wondering where I was. I told myself I'd just sit long enough for my pulse to return to normal. But a wave of exhaustion totaled me. My limbs felt heavy. My head began to nod. I couldn't keep my eyes from drifting closed.

*   *   *

Everything shadowed. The owl hovering over the stone table. Razor-sharp talons and golden eyes. The jackal's high-pitched laughter. Venom dripping from the viper's fangs. The jaguar, claws unsheathed. Hunger that could never be sated. The weasel, crawling so close, its claws scrape the table. Candles burning low, casting shadows on the walls. Golden eyes, green eyes, glittering, intent. All of them fixed on the wolf cub. All of them waiting. The cub's terror, sharp and pungent. The red ruby set in the hilt of the athame, glowing with power. The eagle's scream. And the silver wolf. The one they all wait for. It leaps to the table and opens its great jaws. The cub howls.

"Are you all right?" I felt someone gently shaking my shoulder.

My eyes flew open. The man from the courtyard was standing over me, his eyes shadowed with concern.

"What happened?" he asked.

"I—I must have fallen asleep," I said, feeling shaken and embarrassed. I was soaked with sweat. "I had a dream."

"What sort of dream?"

"Just a bad one." Even though I felt sick and disoriented, I knew I couldn't risk saying more. Especially if the council was right about what the dream meant.

"Dreams are funny," the man said thoughtfully. "They have their own internal logic. They mix past and present and future and then some things that I believe belong to our collective unconscious. Things that may have nothing to do with you specifically."

"Maybe this wasn't specific to me," I agreed. After all, no one had ever explained why I was the one who had this dream, but the fact that I'd had it twice now unnerved me.

I drew in several deep breaths, then got to my feet. So far, so good; walking seemed possible. I glanced at my watch. It was after one. "I'd better find my friend," I said. "Thanks for all your help."

"You're sure you're all right?"

"Yes."

As I started to walk away, he touched me lightly on my arm. "I'm sorry. I haven't even had the manners to ask. What's your name?"

"Morgan," I answered without thinking.

He held out his hand to me. "Well, Morgan, may your magick always bring you joy."

I found Bree on the first floor, holding a tarot deck in a bag. "I was going to send out a search party for you," she said. "We're supposed to meet everyone for lunch in forty-five minutes, remember?"

I bought the book on scrying, and we left the store and headed for the subway station on Spring Street. It was only later, as we emerged from the subway on the Upper West Side, that I thought about the fact that I'd given the man my name. Had I committed some sort of breach of security?

No, I decided. After all, I'd only given him my first name. But I wished I'd thought to ask what his name was.

6

Healing

August 19, 1981

Maeve and I have pledged our souls to each other. We left the village just after dark and went out beneath the cliffs. She and I share an affinity for fire, so it was child's play to kindle a raging bonfire with our minds—the concrete expression of the all-consuming nature of our love. Dancing and licking at the night like an animal, it was a thing of beauty, red and yellow and orange, with a dazzling white-blue heat at its heart. I am so happy, I am nearly delirious. At last I am fully alive.

I even gave her the watch that Da gave to Ma, the one I've carried with me all these years. Funny that I never thought to give it to Grania. But then, I never loved Grania.

There is only one thing more to do. I haven't yet made love to Maeve, though Goddess knows, I want it more than I've ever wanted anything on this earth. But I want no lies between us, so *first I must tell her about Grania and the children. It will be difficult. But our love will get us through. I have no fear. Nothing can quench our fire.*

—Neimhidh

Murray's was a crowded deli on Columbus Avenue, sandwiched between a shop selling computer accessories and a flower stand. The spicy smells of corned beef, pastrami, and sauerkraut suddenly made me realize that I was starving.

Bree and I made our way over to the small, square table where Raven and Robbie sat. Seconds after we pulled up chairs a waitress dropped four huge menus on the table.

"No Sky or Hunter," Raven announced.

"They never showed up at the apartment?" I asked her, starting to worry all over again. I knew Hunter and Sky could take care of themselves, but having the dream a second time had left me with a feeling of dread. Was he just late now, or was he not going to show at all?

"No," Raven answered, "but I recorded a message for them on Bree's dad's answering machine, telling them to get their witchy butts up here."

Bree looked both amused and horrified. "Great. I'm just imagining one of my father's clients calling and getting that message."

The waitress returned. "What'll you have?" she asked.

"Uh—we're waiting for friends," Robbie said. "Could you come back in ten minutes?"

She gestured at the line that had formed near the door. "I got people waiting for tables," she told us. "Either you're ready to order or you should let someone else sit down."

"Let's just order," Bree decided.

So we ordered corned beef and pastrami sandwiches and sodas. Raven got a Reuben. The food came immediately, and I'd eaten half my sandwich when I felt Hunter and Sky nearby. I turned around to see them walking through the door.

Hunter was wearing his leather jacket and a bottle-green scarf. His cheeks were red from the cold. "Sorry we're late," he said as they reached the table.

Raven rolled her eyes. "Nice of you to show up."

Robbie, ever the gentleman, managed to round up two more chairs and bring them over to the table. Sky sat down next to Raven.

"Are you hungry?" I offered Hunter the uneaten half of my sandwich.

"No. Thanks," he said, sounding distracted. He didn't take the chair Robbie had brought for him. Instead, he knelt by my side. "There's something I need to talk to you about," he said in a low voice. "How about if you wrap up your sandwich and we take a walk?"

"I'm full," I said. I was glad of the chance to talk—I wanted to tell him about having the dream again.

I left money for the check and made arrangements to meet the others back at Murray's in half an hour. Then Hunter and I set off. By unspoken agreement we headed toward Central Park, stopping only to buy two takeout coffees, defense against the cold.

We walked down a side street lined with gracious brownstones, past the Dakota, where John Lennon had lived, and finally stopped to sit on a low wall overlooking Strawberry Fields, Lennon's memorial. Because it was so cold, there weren't many visitors to the teardrop-shaped garden that day. But on the circular mosaic imprinted with the word *Imagine* someone had left a bouquet of white and yellow daisies.

"Did you know that Strawberry Field was actually the name of an orphanage next door to John Lennon's boyhood home?" Hunter asked. "His aunt, who raised him, used to threaten to send him there whenever he misbehaved."

"I'll have to remember that tidbit for my dad," I said. "He's still a big fan."

"My parents had all the Beatles' albums," Hunter remembered. "My mum used to play the second side of *Abbey Road* on Sunday mornings. 'Here Comes the Sun.'" He hummed the tune softly for a moment. "Goddess, it's been ages since I thought about that." He shook his head as though trying to shake off the pain of memory.

"At least you know they're alive now," I said, trying to sound positive. The dark wave had demolished Hunter's parents' coven when he was only eight, and his mother and father had been in hiding ever since. For years he hadn't even known for sure whether they were dead or alive. Right before Yule, Hunter's father had actually contacted him through his *lueg*. But the dark wave had overwhelmed the vision, cutting it off before Hunter heard what his father was trying to tell him. Since then we hadn't dared try to contact them again, for fear that it would lead the darkness to them.

"I know they were alive three weeks ago," Hunter corrected, his voice tight. "Or at least Dad was. But anything could have happened since then, and I wouldn't know. That's what kills me—not knowing."

Aching for him, I put my arms around his waist. For the most part Hunter kept his grief for his family hidden well below the surface, but every so often it would well up and I'd see how it always was with him. How part of him would never rest until he knew for certain what had happened to his parents.

I felt a gentle glow of white light in the center of my chest. One of Alyce's healing spells was opening to me. "Will you let me try something?" I asked.

Hunter nodded. I unzipped his jacket halfway. I took off my glove, undid one button of his shirt, and slid my already cold hand against his smooth, warm skin. He flinched, then I felt him opening himself to the white light that was flowing through me.

I began a whispered chant. " 'The heart that loves must one day grieve. Love and grief are the Goddess's twined gifts. Let the pain in, let it open your heart to compassion. Let me help you bear your grief. . . .' "

I couldn't continue. Suddenly I knew exactly what it would feel like to have my parents and Mary K. ripped from me. It was beyond excruciating. It was more than could be borne. I cried out in grief though I managed to keep my hand on Hunter's chest, managed to keep the healing light flowing.

"Shhh," Hunter said. "You don't have to do any more."

"No," I whispered. "I have to finish the spell. 'Then may your heart ease and open to greater love. May the love that flows eternally through the universe embrace and comfort you.' "

Gradually I felt the white light diffusing and, with it, Hunter's pain. My eyes met his. There was something different in them, a new clarity. I felt something that had bound him dissolving. "Thank you," he said.

"Courtesy of Alyce," I told him shakily. "I didn't realize quite how much it hurt. I'm sorry."

He kissed my forehead and pulled me against him. When I'd stopped trembling, he said, "Would you like to know why we're sitting here freezing our bums off instead of eating lunch?"

"Oh, that."

"Yes, that," he said. "First, I'm sorry for not answering your messages. It took us a while to find our contact, and then when we finally tracked him down, he was absolutely terrified. He led us through a maze of elaborate safety precautions. If I'd answered you and he'd noticed, he might have thought I was betraying him."

"It's all right," I said. "I was just worried about you. Did this guy have any information?"

"Yes," Hunter said, "he did."

He paused. The sun, which hadn't been strong that morning, disappeared behind a band of thick, white clouds.

"So?" I prompted after a moment.

Hunter's green eyes looked troubled. "I found out who the leader of the New York Amyranth cell is. Apparently the members of the coven wear masks that represent their animal counterparts when they need to draw on the power of that animal. Their leader wears the wolf's mask. My contact didn't know them all, but he confirmed that there are also coven members who wear the masks of an owl, a viper, a cougar, a jaguar, and a weasel."

"So my dream—"

"Was of the New York cell of Amyranth," Hunter finished. "Yes."

I shuddered. "Hunter, I had the dream again," I told him.

"It was just about an hour ago, while I was in an occult book-store down in SoHo."

"Goddess!" Hunter looked alarmed. "Why didn't you contact me?" Before I could answer, he let out an exclamation of annoyance. "Stupid question. I wasn't answering your messages. Morgan, I'm sorry."

"It's okay," I said. "I mean, it was scary, but this time I knew what it was. I'm not sure why I had it again, though."

"Perhaps because we're in New York," he said. "Or perhaps . . ." He trailed off, looking still more troubled. Then he reached out and took my hand. "There's something I've got to tell you. Something I learned today. It will bring up painful thoughts for you."

Icy fingers of dread walked up my spine as I sensed the weight of whatever news Hunter was carrying. I gave him a weak smile. "Go for it."

"The name of this wolf-masked leader is Ciaran," he said.

"Ciaran?" I felt sick. "It—it can't be the same Ciaran. I mean, surely there's more than one Ciaran in the world."

"I'm sure there is," Hunter agreed. "But this Ciaran is a powerful Woodbane witch in his early forties who comes from northern Scotland. I'm sorry, Morgan, but there really isn't any doubt. He's the one who killed Maeve and Angus."

I realized I'd never had any idea of what happened to Ciaran after he set the fire that killed my parents. "I guess I assumed he was back in Scotland," I said lamely. "But he's here in New York City?"

Hunter nodded, his eyes on my face. I sat there, trying to process this new information. Ciaran—alive. Here. Within my reach.

Within my reach? What the hell did that mean? I asked myself bitterly. What would I do if I ever came face-to-face with him? Turn and run the other way, if I had any brains at all. He'd been more powerful than Maeve and Angus together. He could crush me like an ant.

"We also found out that Ciaran has three children," Hunter went on. "Two of them, Kyle and Iona, still live in Scotland. But the youngest is here in New York. You're not going to believe this." He paused. "It's Killian."

"Killian?" My jaw dropped. "The witch we met last night?"

Hunter nodded grimly. "He was all but sitting in my lap, and I didn't realize he was the one."

I downed the last gulp of my now cold coffee. "That's too much of a coincidence."

"There are no coincidences," Hunter reminded me, stating one of those Wiccan axioms that I found so annoying and cryptic.

I thought of the terrified wolf cub in my dream. "That means Killian is Amyranth's intended victim?"

"That's what it looks like," Hunter said.

"Oh God. First Ciaran kills my mother and father; now he's gunning for his own son."

"Ciaran gave himself to the darkness a long time ago," Hunter said. "It's all of a piece. A man capable of killing the love of his life is capable of killing his own son, too."

"What else did you find out? Do you know where he lives? What he looks like?"

"None of that. I've just told you everything." Hunter crumpled his empty coffee cup and launched it at a trash container a good fifteen feet away. The cup went in.

He hopped down off the wall and helped me off. "I've got to try to find Killian and see if I can suss out why Amyranth wants to drain his power. Maybe he has some sort of special ability they need. In any case, he may have valuable information about the coven, and if I play my cards right, he could become a valuable ally for the council."

"I'm going with you," I said impulsively.

Hunter was suddenly holding my upper arms and scowling at me. "Morgan, are you crazy? You can't come with me—especially now that we know Ciaran is the leader of Amyranth. The last thing I want is for him to become aware of your existence. I wish to God you'd stayed in Widow's Vale. In fact, I should take you to Port Authority right now. You can catch the next bus back upstate. I can bring your car and your things back in a day or so."

In a flash we had reverted to our old antagonistic relationship. "Let go of me," I said, furious. "I don't take orders from you. When I go back to Widow's Vale, I'll be driving my own car, thank you, and I'll go when I'm ready."

For a long moment we just glared at each other. I saw Hunter struggling to keep his temper in check.

"If you stay," he said between his teeth, "you've got to give me your word that you'll keep a low profile. No flashy magick on the street. In fact, while we're in the city, I want you to avoid any magick that isn't absolutely necessary. I don't want you drawing any attention to yourself."

I knew he was right, much as I hated to admit it. "Okay," I said sulkily. "I promise."

"Thank you." Hunter's grasp relaxed.

"Be careful," I said.

He kissed me again. "That's my line. Be careful. I'll see you tonight."

I hurried back to Columbus Avenue. As I neared the restaurant, I passed a father carrying his little son on his shoulders. The boy was laughing, as if it were the greatest treat in the world.

It made me wonder about Killian and his father. Was there ever a time when they were close? What would it be like to be the child of a father who was devoted to evil?

Maybe, I thought, it explained Killian's recklessness. Maybe he was running away from the darkness. That, I thought with a sigh, I could certainly understand.

Bree and the others were on their way out when I got back to Murray's.

"Perfect timing," Bree said as she stepped out of the restaurant. "Do you want to come to the Museum of Modern Art with me and Sky?"

"I opted out," Raven said. "I'm going to see a movie down in the Village." I didn't know Raven well enough to be sure, but she was talking more loudly than usual, and I had a feeling it meant that things between her and Sky were still tense.

I glanced at Robbie. He looked so miserable, I was certain that he hadn't been invited on the museum trip. I tried to remember: Was Bree always this ruthless in relationships? Or was Robbie getting special treatment because he was the one she actually cared about? Either way, her behavior made me uncomfortable.

"No thanks," I said, my voice curt. "I'm not in the mood."

Bree shrugged. "Okay, we'll see you back at the apartment."

I started for Broadway. Since I was unexpectedly on my own, it occurred to me that now would be a good time to see if I could find Maeve and Angus's old apartment. I thought of the promise I'd made Hunter, to refrain from anything that might draw unwelcome attention to me. But looking for my birth parents' old apartment wouldn't do that, I reasoned. I'd just have to make sure I avoided using magick during the search.

A ray of late-afternoon sun emerged from the clouds as I walked, and that bit of brightness seemed to lift the mood on the street. Two skateboarders whizzed by while a woman assured her reluctant poodle that it was a beautiful day for a walk. I suddenly realized that Robbie was trailing behind me.

"Robbie," I said. "Where are you going?"

Robbie gave an overly casual shrug. "I thought I'd hang with you. Is that okay?"

Robbie looked so miserable and abandoned that I couldn't say no. Besides, Robbie was special. He'd been with me when I found Maeve's tools.

"I'm not going to a very scenic part of the city," I warned. "Um—I was kind of trying to keep this quiet. You know, discreet."

Robbie raised his eyebrows. "What, are you going to score some dope or something?"

I swatted him on the shoulder. "Idiot. Of course not. It's just . . . Maeve and Angus had an apartment in Hell's Kitchen before they moved upstate. I want to find it."

"Okay," Robbie said. "I don't know what the big secret is, but I'll keep my mouth shut."

We walked on in silence. I was the one who finally broke it. "I think your restraint is admirable," I told him. "If I were you, I would have decked Bree a long time ago."

He grinned at me. "You did once, didn't you?"

I winced at the memory of a horrible argument in the hallway at school. An argument about Cal. "I slapped her across the face," I corrected him. "Actually, it felt awful."

"Yeah, that's what I figured."

I tried to think of a delicate way to put my question. "Did things go—okay—between you two last night?"

Robbie took a deep breath. "That's what's so weird. It was great. I mean, as great as it could be with Raven snoring right next to us. We just cuddled. And it felt good to be together, totally warm and affectionate—and right. It was sweet, Morgan, for both of us, I swear."

"So, what changed this morning?" I asked.

"I don't have a clue. I woke up, said good morning to Bree when I saw her in the kitchen, and she snapped my head off. I can't figure out what I did."

I thought about it as we waited at the bus stop. I wondered how much I could tell Robbie without betraying what Bree had told me. After about ten minutes of waiting, a bus finally lumbered to a stop. We managed to snag seats together, facing the center aisle.

"Maybe you didn't do anything wrong," I said, grateful for the blasting heat. I loosened my scarf and peeled off my gloves. "Or maybe what you did wrong last night was to be right."

Robbie massaged his forehead. "You just lost me."

"Okay, maybe last night things were every bit as great as

you thought they were," I said. "And maybe that's the problem. When things are good is when Bree has trouble trusting them. So that's when she has to mess them up again."

"That makes absolutely no sense," Robbie said.

I gave him a look. "Did I ever claim Bree was logical?"

We got off at Forty-ninth Street and began walking west. "We're looking for number seven-eight-eight," I told Robbie.

He glanced up at the building we were passing. "We're nowhere near."

We waited for the light on Ninth Avenue to turn. Ninth Avenue looked pretty decent, with lots of restaurants and small shops selling ethnic foods. But as we kept walking west, Forty-ninth Street became seedier and seedier. The theaters and little studio workshops were gone now. Garbage was piled by the curb. The buildings were mostly residential tenement types, with crumbling brickwork and boarded-up windows. Many were spray-painted with gang tags. We were in Hell's Kitchen.

I knew that this neighborhood had a long history of violent crime. Robbie was wide-eyed and wary. I cast my senses, hoping to pick up any trace Maeve might have left. At first all I got were flashes of the people in the neighborhood: families in crowded apartments; a few elderly people, ailing and miserably alone; a crack junkie, adrenaline rocketing through her body. Then I felt the hairs along the back of my neck rise. In the worn brickwork of an abandoned building I saw vestiges of runes and magickal symbols, nearly covered over by layers of graffiti. It didn't feel like Maeve's or Angus's work. That made sense; they had renounced their powers completely when they fled Ireland. But it was proof that witches had been here.

"This is it," Robbie said as we came to a soot-streaked redbrick tenement with iron fire escapes running down its front. The building was narrow and only five stories high. It seemed sad and neglected, and I wondered how much worse it had gotten since Maeve and Angus had lived in it nearly twenty years ago.

I couldn't pick up any trace of my birth mother, but that didn't mean there wasn't something inside the building. If only I could get into the actual apartment where she'd lived. Three low stairs led to a front door behind a steel-mesh gate. A sign on a first-floor window read Apartments for Rent, Powell Mgmt. Co. I rang the bell marked Superintendent and waited.

No one answered the bell or my pounding on the steel gate. Robbie said, "Now what?"

I could try a spell, I thought. But I wasn't supposed to use magick unless I absolutely had to. And this didn't qualify as an emergency.

"Can I use your phone?" I asked Robbie. I called the management company on Robbie's cell phone. To my astonishment, the woman on the phone told me that apartment three was available. I was so excited, my voice shook as I made an appointment to see the place the next day. It was meant to be, I thought. Obviously.

"I hate to bring this up," Robbie said when I hung up. "But you look like the high school kid you are. I mean, why would anyone show you an apartment?"

"I'm not sure," I told Robbie. "But I'll find a way."

7

The Watch

August 20, 1981

This morning at dawn I took Maeve for a walk along the cliffs. We were both still floating on the joy of last night. Yet I knew I had to tell her. I expected it to shock, possibly hurt her, but I was certain she'd forgive me in the end. After all, we are mùirn beatha dàns.

Maeve was going on about where we'd live. Much as she loves Ballynigel, she does not want to stay here her entire life; she wants to see the world, and I would love nothing more than to show it to her. But her happy ramblings were like blows to my heart. At last, when I could stand to wait no more, I told her, as gently as I could, that I was not yet free to travel with her, that I had a wife and two children in Scotland.

At first she only looked at me in confusion. I repeated what I'd said, this time taking her hands in mine.

Then her confusion was replaced by disbelief. She begged me, weeping, to tell her it wasn't true. But I couldn't. I could not lie to her.

I pulled her close to kiss away her tears. But she would have none of me. She yanked her hands from mine and stepped away. I pleaded with her to give me time. I told her I couldn't afford to enrage Greer—not if I wanted to take her place. But I swore I'd leave the lot of them as soon as I could.

She cut me off. "You will not leave your wife and children," she said, the anguish in her eyes turning to fire. "First you betray me with lies. Now you want to destroy a family as well?" Then she told me to leave her, to get away.

I couldn't believe she was serious. I argued, cajoled, begged. I told her to take time to consider. I said we'd find a gentle way to go forward together, that, of course, I would provide for my family. But no matter what I said, I could not dissuade her. She who had been so soft, so yielding, was suddenly like iron.

My soul is shattered. Tomorrow I return to Scotland.

—Neimhidh

When we got back to Ninth Avenue, Robbie took off on his own. I went back to Bree's father's place. We hadn't made any group plans for the evening, and the apartment was empty. For a while I couldn't settle down. I was too revved up—from the news about Ciaran being here in the city, from having found Maeve's old building. Was the watch still there? I wondered. If it was, would I be able to find it? I tried to scry for it, but I was too wired to concentrate. Finally I curled up with the book on scrying that I'd bought in SoHo and read for a while.

The sun had almost set when I sensed Hunter walking down the hall. I couldn't quite believe my luck. Were we really going to have a chance to be alone together in the apartment? I rushed into the bathroom and quickly brushed my teeth and my hair.

But the moment Hunter opened the door, I realized this was not going to be a romantic interlude. He walked in, took off his scarf and jacket, gave me a curt nod, then went to stare morosely out the window.

I went to stand beside him. Despite his mood, I immediately tuned in to our connection. I couldn't have defined either of them, but this was completely different from my connection with the man in the bookstore. Hunter touched everything in me. It was a delicious tease to stand near him, not physically touching, and let myself feel how his presence stroked my every nerve ending into a state of total anticipation.

He reached out and caught my hand in his. "Don't," he said gently. "I can't be with you that way right now."

"What happened?" I asked, feeling a twinge of alarm. "What went wrong?"

"My finding Killian. I didn't. Either he got wind of the fact that a council Seeker is looking for him or Amyranth has already snatched him because I can't find him anywhere."

"Did you try—"

Hunter began to pace the length of the living room. "I

found his flat, rang his doorbell and his phone. I went to the club, found out the names of some of his friends, and asked them. I've sent him witch messages. He doesn't answer any of them. I even took out my *lueg* and scryed right on the street. That's how desperate I was for a lead—any lead. And none of it has done a bit of good," he finished bitterly.

He dropped onto the couch and ran a hand through his hair. "I simply don't know where to go next with this. I'm going to have to contact the council again."

"Want me to try scrying?"

"I've scryed my way to Samhain and back again and I haven't seen a trace of Killian."

"I know. But I scry with fire," I reminded him. "I might get a different result."

He shrugged and reached for a thick, ivory candle on the coffee table—one that Bree must have bought the day before—and pushed it toward me. "Be my guest," he said, but his voice was skeptical.

I settled myself cross-legged on the floor. I focused on my breathing, but my thoughts didn't slip away as easily as they usually did. I wondered if I'd be able to transfer what I'd done with the crystal to fire. Whether this time I'd be able to control the vision.

"Morgan?"

"Sorry," I said. "I got distracted. Let me try again. You want to see where Killian is right now?"

"That'd be a start."

"Okay." Again I focused on my breathing. This time I felt my mind quieting and the tension draining from my muscles. I stared at the candle's wick, thought of fire, and the candle lit. I let my eyes focus on the flame, sinking deeper into my meditative state until the coffee table, the room, Hunter, even the candle itself faded from my consciousness. There was only the flame.

Killian. I let a picture of him as he'd been at the club fill my mind—confident, cocky, laughing, with that heady mix of danger and delight in his own power.

I focused on the fire, asked it to give me the vision that I sought, to show me Killian as he was right now. I asked it to let me in, and I sent my energy toward it. I couldn't touch it the way I'd touched the crystal. The fire would burn me. But I let my power flicker beside it, calling to its heat and energy.

Something inside the flame shifted. It danced higher, blazed brighter. Its blue center became a mirror, and in it I saw Killian in profile. He was alone in a dark, dilapidated room. There was a window across from him, casting reddish light across his face. Through the window I could see some sort of gray stone tower, partly cloaked by a screen of bare tree branches. Killian seemed frightened, his face pale and drawn.

I sent more of my power to the flame, willing more of the vision to appear, something that would give a clue to his location. The flame crackled, and Killian turned and looked straight into my eyes. Abruptly, the connection was severed. I pushed back a surge of annoyance and focused on the flame again. Again I asked for the vision of Killian as he was now and sent my energy to dance with the flame.

This time there was no vision. Instead, the flame winked out, almost as if someone had snuffed it. I blinked hard. The rest of the room came back into focus.

Hunter was watching me, his eyes inscrutable. "I saw him," he said in an odd tone. "And I wasn't joining my power to yours. I've never been able to do that before, see the vision of the one who's scrying."

"Is that a problem?" I asked uncertainly.

"No," he said. "It's because your scrying is so powerful." He pulled me up on the couch beside him and wrapped his arms around me. "You are a seer." He kissed each of my eyelids. "And I'm awed. Even humbled—almost."

"Almost?" I couldn't help being thrilled that I'd managed to pull off a feat of magick that had stymied Hunter.

"Well, you know, humble isn't exactly my style," he confessed with a grin.

"I've noticed."

"Nor is it Killian's," he said, his tone serious again. He blew out a breath and leaned back against the couch. "At least we know he's alive. He didn't seem hurt, either. He looked scared, though. That room he was in, do you have any sense of where it is?"

I shook my head. "None."

"I wonder," Hunter said, "why the vision was snuffed out so quickly and why it didn't come back. It's almost as if someone didn't want you to see."

"Maybe Killian himself," I said. "He looked at me, remember? Maybe he felt me scrying for him. Do you think he's got enough power to cut off a vision?"

"I'd guess that he's not lacking in power," Hunter said with a sigh.

"There's got to be a way to find him," I said.

"Hang on a minute," Hunter said. "The window across

from him. Did you notice the church steeple you could see through it?"

"Oh!" I exclaimed. "That's what it was."

"Yes. And there was reddish light on his face, so I'm pretty sure the window must have been a westerly one. Also, wherever he is must be far enough west that the sunset isn't blocked by lots of tall buildings."

"Wow." I was impressed by his deductions.

He looked intent, eager. "I'm thinking maybe I could find a building that satisfies those conditions—far west, with a westerly window, opposite a gray stone church."

"That sounds like a lot of legwork."

"Maybe tomorrow I can come up with a way to narrow the search. Listen, there's one more contact I want to try to track down tonight. I'm not sure when I'll get back."

I glanced at my watch. It was six. "Are you telling me not to wait up?"

Hunter looked genuinely regretful. "I'm afraid so." He put on his jacket and scarf and kissed me. "I'll be back as soon as I can."

Robbie was the first to show up at the apartment. After we'd split up, he'd gone down to the Village, where he'd dropped in on one of the chess shops near Washington Square Park. "Got beat by a seventy-year-old grand master," he reported with a satisfied grin. "It was an education."

Bree, Raven, and Sky showed up a few minutes after Robbie—Raven must have hooked up with the other two at some point during the afternoon. Bree was irritable and out of sorts, but Raven and Sky seemed to be getting along again. We ordered Chinese food, and then Raven and Sky went out to look up some goth friends of Raven's while Robbie, Bree, and I watched a Hong Kong action movie on pay-per-view. An exciting Friday night in the big city.

Whenever it was that Hunter returned to the apartment, I was asleep.

On Saturday morning I woke up before Bree. Raven wasn't in the room; extending my senses, I realized that she was in the study with Sky. Quietly I pulled on jeans and a sweater. I found Hunter in the kitchen, washing up a plate and cup. "Morning," he said. "Want me to make you a cup of tea before I go?"

"You know better," I said, and reached into the fridge for a Diet Coke.

"Ugh," he said. "Well, I'm off on a long day of looking for gray stone churches and westerly windows."

"It sounds like it could take you a week," I said. "There must be hundreds of churches like that in the city."

He shrugged, looking resigned. "What else can I do? Whether Killian is hiding his own tracks or someone else is doing it for him, I'm not getting anywhere trying to find him by magick." He picked up his jacket. "What are you going to do today?" he asked.

I helped myself to one of the Pop-Tarts that Bree had thoughtfully stocked up on and tried to look nonchalant. "Robbie and I thought we'd wander around the city for a while." It wasn't a lie—I knew better than that with Hunter. But it wasn't the whole truth, either.

Hunter gave me a searching look but didn't question me further. "I'll see you this evening for our circle," he said.

*　　*　　*

"We'll be the perfect young couple," Robbie said as we walked down Forty-ninth Street. "I mean, you've got a ring and everything." He glanced at the fake diamond ring we'd just bought at a tacky gift shop and shook his head. "Whoa. It's a little freaky to see that thing on you."

"Yeah, well, imagine how I feel wearing it," I said.

Robbie laughed. "Just think what a promising future we're in for, starting out in a tenement apartment in Hell's Kitchen."

"That's all Maeve and Angus started with in this country," I said. I felt suddenly very sad. "The entries from her Book of Shadows at that time were all about how she couldn't bear living in the city. She thought it was full of unhappy people, racing around pointlessly."

"Well, it is, sort of." Robbie gave me a sympathetic glance. "And didn't they come here straight after Ballynigel was destroyed? Of course she was depressed. She'd just lost her home, her family, nearly everyone she loved."

"And she'd given up her magick," I added. "She said it was like living in a world suddenly stripped of all its colors. It makes me sad for her."

We reached the building. It seemed even more dilapidated today. Robbie grinned at me. "Well, Ms. Rowlands. Are you ready for your first real estate experience?"

"Hey, my mom is a Realtor," I reminded him. "I probably know more about leases than the rental agent."

Still, I could feel my heart race as I rang the super's bell. I was about to see my birth parents' apartment! What would it be like? Would I be able to find the watch?

"Who is it?" asked a woman's voice over a crackly intercom.

"It's Morgan and Robbie Rowlands," I called back. "I spoke to the management company yesterday about the apartment for rent. They said you would show it to me today at noon."

Robbie tapped his watch. We were on time.

"All right," she said after a hesitation. "I'll be right there."

We waited another five minutes before the steel gate was opened to reveal a short, heavyset woman in her late sixties. I could see the pink of her scalp through gray pin curls.

She looked at me and Robbie, and I saw the suspicion in her eyes.

"The apartment's this way," she grumbled.

We followed her up a flight of stairs and down a narrow hallway. The paint was peeling, and the place reeked of urine. I hoped it hadn't been this bad when Maeve and Angus lived here. I couldn't bear the thought of my mother, who'd had such a profound love of the earth, walking into this ugliness every day.

The woman took a ring of keys from the pocket of her housedress and opened a door with the number two on it. "The rent's six-seventy-five a month," she told us. "You don't find prices like that in Manhattan anymore. Better grab it fast."

"Actually, we came to see apartment three," I said. "The management company said it was available."

She gave me a look that reminded me of the look I'd gotten from the clerk in the records office. "They were wrong. I got someone living in apartment three," she said. "It's not for rent. This one is. Do you want to see it or not?"

Robbie and I exchanged glances. I was fighting intense disappointment. All this for nothing. We weren't going to get into Maeve's apartment. I wasn't going to find the watch after all.

"We'll look at it," Robbie said. As the woman lumbered toward the stairs, he nudged me and whispered, "I didn't want this woman realizing we were poseurs and calling the police or something."

She let us into a dark, railroad-flat apartment, not much wider than the narrow hallway. "This is your living room," she said as we entered a small front room. She tapped the steel bars that covered the window. "Security," she told us proudly.

The kitchen had a claw-foot bathtub, a small refrigerator desperately in need of cleaning, and a family of large, healthy cockroaches living in the sink. "Just put down some boric acid," the woman said casually.

Then she took us into the last room, a tiny decrepit bedroom with a window the size of a phone directory.

"You two got jobs?"

"I work in . . . with computers," Robbie said.

"I waitress," I said. That had been Maeve's first job in America.

"Well, you'll have to put all that in the application," the woman said. "Come down to my apartment and you can fill one out."

I was wondering how we were going to get out of the application process when I felt something in the tiny bedroom calling me. I studied the stained ceiling.

"There used to be a leak," the woman admitted, her gaze following mine. "But we fixed it."

But that wasn't what had caught my attention. I had felt a magickal pull from the corner of the ceiling. Looking more closely, I saw that one of the panels of the dropped ceiling was slightly askew. Whatever I was sensing was behind that panel. The watch? Could it possibly be, after all these years? I had to find out.

"I told you, we fixed the leak," the woman said loudly.

I bit back an irritated reply. I needed a moment of privacy. How was I going to get rid of this woman?

Frustrated, I raised my eyebrows at Robbie and nodded toward the living room. Robbie shot me a "Who, me?" look.

I nodded again, more emphatically.

"Um—could I ask you a question about the living room?" Robbie said hesitantly. "It's about the woodwork."

"What woodwork?" the woman demanded, but she followed him, anyway.

As soon as they had left the room, I shut the door and quickly turned the lock. I had to reach that ceiling panel. There was only one way. I climbed up on the narrow window ledge and balanced precariously.

Thank the Goddess for low ceilings! I thought as I found I could just reach the panel. With my fingertips I pushed up against it. The panel moved a fraction of an inch. I stretched and pressed harder. The magickal pull was getting stronger. I felt a faint warm current against my hand. I stretched, groaned softly, and gave another hard push.

The panel lifted up and I fell off the ledge onto the floor with a thud.

"Ow," I mumbled. Quickly I climbed back up onto the ledge. I heard the superintendent's footsteps hurrying across the apartment. Then she was twisting the doorknob, trying to open the door.

"Hey, what's going on in there?" she yelled, pounding on the door. "What are you doing? Are you okay?"

"I'm sure she's fine," Robbie said quickly.

"Then come out of there!" the woman shouted, pounding harder.

Just ignore her, I told myself, heart racing. I stuck my fingers through the open panel. Empty space and a wooden beam. Then my fingers closed on smooth fabric encasing something hard and round.

"You come out right now or I'm calling the police!" the woman shouted.

I didn't hesitate. This was absolutely necessary magick. If he ever found out, Hunter would understand.

"You will forget," I whispered. "You never saw us. This did not happen. You will forget."

It was as simple as that. One moment the woman was screaming and threatening, the next I heard her ask Robbie, "So you want to see the apartment? You know, you're the first one I've shown it to."

I put the panel back in place, then jumped down from the ledge, clutching the watch. Apartment three must be directly upstairs, I realized. Maeve must have hidden the watch beneath her floorboards. I unfolded the green silk and felt a protective spell whispering from the material. The watch case was gold, engraved with a Celtic knot pattern. A white face, gold hands. A tiny cabochon ruby on the end of the winding stem. I stared at it, and tears rose in my eyes. It represented so many things to me, things both wonderful and horrible.

But there was no time to think about that now. I tucked the watch into my pocket and unlocked the door. Then I went out to get Robbie.

"You're not going to believe what I found in there!" I said when we were about a block away from the apartment. "You've got to see this watch." I started to take it from my pocket.

Robbie was walking fast, his eyes on the sidewalk. "Just put it away," he said.

"What?" I was startled at his angry tone.

"I don't want to see it," he snapped.

I stared at him. "What's wrong?" I asked. "Is this about Bree?"

Robbie turned on me, his eyes blazing. "No, Morgan. This is about you. What the hell happened back there? One minute that old lady was calling for you to get out of the bedroom. The next minute she couldn't remember ever having seen us before."

"I did a little spell," I said. "I made her forget."

"You did what?"

"Robbie, it's okay," I said. "It was temporary. It's already worn off."

"How do you know that?" he demanded. "How do you know that spell didn't rewire her brain? How do you know she won't think she's going senile when she suddenly remembers the two people she blanked on? Elderly people find that kind of thing a little upsetting."

"I know because I made the spell," I said, keeping my voice calm. "What are you so freaked about, anyway?"

Robbie looked enraged. "You don't get it, do you? You messed with someone's mind! You've lucked into these amazing powers, and you're abusing them. How do I know you won't do something like that to me?"

I felt like he'd knocked the wind out of me. When I found my voice, it sounded high and tinny. "Because I gave you my word that I wouldn't. Come on, Robbie, we've been friends since second grade. You know I'm not like that. This was a special circumstance."

He looked at me like I was a stranger, a stranger who frightened him. "The Morgan I know wouldn't screw around with some poor old lady. You played her like she was a puppet. And I feel like a jerk for having been part of that whole charade. I feel dirty."

I tried to calm the butterflies in my stomach. This was serious. "Robbie, I'm sorry," I said. "I had no right to make you part of that. But this watch belonged to Maeve. I had to get it. Did you really think I could leave it there? It was my mother's. That makes it my birthright."

"Like your power?" he asked, his voice shaking.

"Yes. Exactly like my power." Every so often words come out of your mouth with a cool, resonant certainty and you know you've hit a bone-deep truth. There's no taking it back or denying it. That's how it felt then, and Robbie and I both stood there, suspended for a moment in the awful implications of what I'd just said.

Maeve had given up her magick, but there was nothing on this earth that would make me give up mine.

"So this birthright of yours." I could see him fighting for control, trying to keep his voice steady. "It gives you the right to manipulate some woman you don't even know?"

"I didn't say that!"

"No, it's just what you *did*. You were flexing your power. Well, I'm starting to think maybe your power isn't such a great thing."

"Robbie, that's not true! I—"

"Forget it," he said. "I'm going to see if I can get in on another chess game. If I'm going to be totally overwhelmed, at least it's going to be by something I understand."

He stalked off down Ninth Avenue, leaving me with Maeve's watch and a sick feeling in the pit of my stomach.

8

Spy

August 27, 1981

I've been back in Scotland almost a week now. And a bleak, colorless landscape it is. Was I ever happy here? Grania met me at the door with bawling babies clinging to her skirts and a list of complaints. It had been pouring for ten days straight, and the thatching on the roof was leaking, making the entire house reek of mildew. Oh, and little Iona was cutting a tooth and couldn't I make a tincture for the pain? It's a wonder she didn't ask me to stop the rains. The thing is, Grania's not without power of her own. Before the babies came, she was a promising witch. But now she's the martyr, and it's all up to me. I wasn't home half an hour before I left for the pub, and I've spent most of my time there ever since. I can't face my own home. Can't face life without Maeve.

Last night was the worst yet. The little ones both had a bug. Kyle was feverish. Iona couldn't keep down anything she ate. With Greer still in Ballynigel, I was called on to lead a circle. I came back to find Grania shrieking like a harpy. How could I have left her with two sick kids? Didn't I care about my own children? I didn't have it in me to lie. "No," I told her. "Nor do I care for you, you fat cow." She struck me then, and I nearly struck her back. Instead, I told her she was a shrew and a chore just to look at. Made her cry, which of course drove me even farther round the bend. Finally I took her to bed just to get her to stop the waterworks. It was awful. All I wanted was Maeve in my arms.

Today Grania's playing the victim for all it's worth, and I find myself wishing I could stop her pathetic whining once and for all. It would cost me the coven, though. She's still Greer's daughter, with a certain inherited position here, no matter how undeserved.

I have so much rage in me that everything I see is enclosed in an aura of flaming red. I am furious with Maeve for her self-righteous rejection of me. Furious with myself for marrying Grania, when I should have known Maeve was out there, waiting for me. And furious with Grania for having the wretched luck to be who she is.

She just came in to tell me that she already feels a child stirring within her from last night's mockery of lovemaking. "It *will be a boy," she said, a sickly hope on her face. "What shall we name him?"*

"We shall call him Killian," I answered. It means strife.

—Neimhidh

I was grateful no one else was in the apartment when I got back. I was still trying to pull myself together after Robbie's accusations. After the shock had come anger. How could he have thought I'd hurt that old woman? How could he accuse me of such awful things? I'd assumed Robbie was strong enough not to be freaked by things he didn't understand. Instead, he'd gotten totally hysterical. He hadn't even listened when I'd tried to explain.

Yet I couldn't help feeling a twinge—more than a twinge—of guilt. There'd been some truth in what Robbie had said. Plus I'd broken my promise to Hunter to keep a low profile.

I drew out the watch that Ciaran had given to Maeve. The gold case gleamed softly in the light coming through the living room windows. I pulled out the ruby-tipped winding stem and wound it to the right, deasil, feeling the resistance of the spring inside. Would it work after all these years? Yes, there was a soft, even ticking.

Had it been worth my trouble? I wondered, thinking about the argument with Robbie. Yes. I could no more have left the watch in that awful apartment than I could have left Maeve's Book of Shadows in Selene's house.

Sitting cross-legged on Bree's father's couch, I tried to find a way through the murk. I wasn't going to lose Robbie, I told myself. Especially now that I'd sort of lost Bree. We both needed to calm down, and we probably both needed to apologize. And Robbie needed to realize that I was still the same Morgan he knew and trusted.

But you're not, a voice inside me said. You're a blood witch, and no one but another blood witch will ever understand.

Again I thought about why I'd wanted the watch so badly. Was it simply because it had been loved by Maeve? Or was I fascinated by the fact that it had been given to her by Ciaran, her *mùirn beatha dàn*, the man who eventually became her murderer? I felt my jaw tensing with anger as I thought of him, and I had to will myself to relax.

Then my senses tingled. Hunter was approaching. I took a few deep breaths to calm my conflicted heart. I wasn't ready to discuss this with Hunter, both because I was certain he'd side with Robbie and because I knew he wouldn't approve of my having anything connected to Ciaran.

I tucked the watch away in my pocket and went to the door. "Hey," I said as he came in. "How was the rest of your day?"

Hunter pulled me to him. "Spectacularly lousy. How was yours?"

"So-so. You didn't find that building?"

"Not yet, no. I'm going to keep looking. I just wanted to stop in and tell you I wouldn't be here for tonight's circle." Hunter arched one blond eyebrow. "Anyone else here?"

"Nope. Just you and me."

"Thank the Goddess for that," he said. He held me tight, and I felt that familiar shift as our energies aligned in perfect synchronicity. "Mmm," I said. "This is nice. I think I've had enough of the group experience."

Hunter laughed. "You didn't expect we'd get on each other's nerves living in such close quarters? Try growing up in a coven where everyone's been able to read your emotions from the day you were born. There's a reason New York is teeming with witches run away from home."

He took off his jacket, and we went into the kitchen. I got myself a Diet Coke from the fridge.

Hunter wrinkled his nose. "How can you drink that vile stuff?"

"It's delicious. And nutritious."

"You would think so," he said darkly. He sighed. "I'm up against a brick wall, Morgan. Killian was here, and now he's gone. I've been—what do they say? Not beating the bushes."

"Pounding the pavement?" I suggested helpfully.

"Whatever. Not a trace of him anywhere. It's almost as if he never existed." Hunter ran himself a glass of water from the tap. "I didn't imagine him, did I?"

"If you did, then we shared the same arrogant hallucination."

A corner of Hunter's mouth lifted. "You didn't find him—attractive?"

"No," I said, realizing with some surprise that I was being totally honest, not trying to save Hunter's feelings. "I liked him. I thought he was fun. But he also seemed kind of stuck on himself."

"Personally, I think he's a pain, but that doesn't mean he isn't worth saving."

"That's big of you," I teased, but the worried look in Hunter's eyes scared me. "You think Amyranth has him already, don't you?"

He didn't reply, but his lips thinned.

"Look, why don't we just put off the circle for a night?" I suggested. "We could all help you search for him."

Hunter's answer was swift and firm. "No. Especially now that we know Ciaran's involved. I don't want you anywhere near this."

"Do you think he already knows about me? I mean, that Maeve and Angus had a daughter."

Hunter looked absolutely miserable. "God, I hope not."

I took some deep breaths and tried to fight off the feeling of dread.

I felt Hunter's hand close around my wrist. "I'm going to leave soon. But first . . . come with me. Let's just . . . be with each other for a little while."

I nodded. We went into the guest bedroom and lay down on my narrow mattress. I let Hunter hold me loosely in his arms. I wanted to clasp him to me, to stave off all the desperation and fear charging through me. I wanted never to let him go.

"We can't hold on to each other forever, you know," he said, echoing my thoughts.

"Why not?" I asked. "Why can't we just stay here and keep each other safe?"

He kissed the tip of my nose. "For one thing, I'm a Seeker. For another, none of us can guarantee another's safety, much as we'd love to." He kissed me again, this time on the mouth. I could feel his heart beating against mine. Someday, I thought, when all this is over, we'll be able to be like this all the time. Warm, close together.

Someday.

*   *   *

By the time I'd changed, set out candles and salt, and puri-
fied the living room with the smoke of cedar and sage, Hunter
was gone and everyone else had returned to the apartment.

Though Bree and Robbie seemed to be keeping their
distance, Sky and Raven had come in together. Packages were
put away. Plans for later that evening were discussed. When
everyone had finally settled in, we gathered in the living room
for our circle. It felt odd to be there without Jenna, Matt,
Ethan, Sharon, and the other members of Kithic. I wondered
briefly what they were doing back in Widow's Vale.

Since Sky was the only initiated witch among us, she
would lead the circle. But first, at Hunter's request, I filled
everyone in on the Killian situation.

"Let's work a spell to lift obstacles and send power to
Hunter," Sky suggested.

We pushed the few pieces of furniture against the walls
and rolled up the rug. Sky traced a wide circle with chalk on
the wood floor. On each of the four compass points she
placed one of the four elements: a small dish of water for
water, a stick of incense for air, a crystal for earth, and a candle for fire. One by one, we entered the circle. Sky closed it
behind us.

"We come together to honor the Goddess and the God,"
she began. "We ask their help and guidance. May our magick
be pure and strong, and may we use it to help those in need."

We joined hands, each of us focusing on our breathing. Bree
stood on one side of me, Robbie on the other. I opened my
senses. I could feel the familiar presences of the others, feel
their heartbeats. They were all precious to me, I realized. Even

Raven. The circle bound us as allies in the fight against darkness.

Slowly we began to move deasil. I felt power moving through me. I drew energy up from the earth and down from the sky.

Sky had us visualize the rune Thorn, for overcoming adversity. Then she led us in a chant for lifting obstacles. The circle began to move faster. I could feel the energy humming, rising, flowing among us, getting stronger. Sky's pale face was alight with the purity of the power she was channeling. She traced a sigil in the air, and I felt the power lift and rise above the circle.

"To Hunter," she said.

Abruptly the air changed. The thrum of power was gone. Suddenly we seemed like a bunch of teenagers, standing around a New York City living room instead of the beings of power we'd been just moments before.

"Good work," Sky said, sounding pleased. "Everyone, sit down for a moment. Ground yourselves."

We all sat down on the floor.

"Something real happened there," Robbie said.

Bree looked worried. "How do we know that energy went to Hunter and didn't get picked up by the Woodbanes?"

"I bound it with a sigil of protection before I sent it out," Sky answered.

"So now he should be able to find Killian?" Raven asked.

Sky shrugged her slender shoulders. "There are no guarantees, of course. Killian seems to have a gift for making himself scarce. But hopefully what we just did will make it a little easier for Hunter." She glanced around at the circle. "We'd better clean up."

For the next twenty minutes we cleaned up and debated

what everyone was going to do with the rest of the evening. Raven wanted to go to another club—a normal, nonwitch one, this time—while Robbie wanted to hear some obscure band that was playing in Tribeca, and Bree wanted to go to a trendy pool hall down near Battery Park. I, of course, was wondering if Hunter was going to show up, but it seemed wimpy to say that aloud. And I was tired. Maybe it was the fight with Robbie or the circle, but I felt drained.

We were still trying to make a plan when the apartment door opened and Hunter walked in, one hand gripping Killian's elbow. Killian looked sullen, and Hunter looked irritated. It was clear that Killian had not come of his own free will.

We must all have been staring openmouthed because Killian's sullen expression turned to one of delight. He grinned and said, "I am pretty amazing, aren't I?"

"Are you all right?" I asked, unable to reconcile his cheerful presence with the Killian of my vision.

"Tip-top," Killian replied. "How about you, love?" He flicked his thumb at Hunter. "Must be rough, hanging out with Mr. Doom-and-Gloom here. Sucks the joy right out of life."

"Shut up and sit down," Hunter snapped.

Killian first helped himself to a soda from the fridge and then flopped onto the couch.

"He was in Chelsea," Hunter said, "hiding out in an abandoned apartment building."

"Who said anything about hiding?" Killian protested. "I just wanted some time by myself. No one asked you to come barging in, Seeker."

"Would you rather your father found you first?" Hunter snapped.

Killian gave an overly casual shrug. "Why should I care if my father finds me? As long as he doesn't try to send me to bed early." He held up his hand as Hunter started to speak. "And please, don't start up with that idiocy about him wanting to drain my power. I mean, honestly, where do you get all this? Is that what the council spends its time on—dreaming up daft conspiracy theories?"

I couldn't make sense of it. Had my vision been all wrong? Or had Killian been held somewhere and escaped? Was Killian powerful enough to manipulate my scrying?

Hunter glanced at Bree. "Do you think your father would mind if Killian stayed the night?"

"I guess not," Bree said, but she didn't look happy about it.

"Right, then," Hunter said. "He can sleep in the living room with me and Robbie."

"Oh, joy," Killian caroled.

Robbie dug out another green stuff sack from the mound of gear in the living room and tossed it to him. Killian caught the air mattress, then dropped it on the floor and fixed his gaze on Raven. "I knew we'd meet again. How about if you and I sneak off for a quick pint, get to know each other better?"

"That's enough," Sky said.

Killian shrugged and grinned at me. "Touchy bunch you hang out with. Everyone always taking offense. Are you as bad as the rest of them?"

"Are you playing us off against each other?" I asked, not able to muster quite as much outrage as I should have. There was just something about him that appealed to me. I felt like we were coconspirators. It was a completely alien feeling for me, but I liked it.

Killian's grin grew even wider. "Well, it would provide a little drama."

"Oh, I think you have plenty of drama in your life," Hunter said. "Anyway, you're not going anywhere tonight. I worked too hard to find you—I'm not going to risk you running off or getting captured."

"As if you knew anything about it," Killian said with contempt.

"Would you excuse us for a minute?" I said, motioning for Hunter and Sky to follow me into the study for a quick huddle.

"I think you all ought to go out and leave me here with Killian," I said.

"Are you mad?" Hunter demanded.

"He and I kind of . . . get along," I said. "I don't understand it," I added quickly, "but he's not flirting with me, the way he does with Raven. Bree and Sky both flat-out dislike him. And Hunter, the two of you just irritate each other. I think I might be able to get him to talk if you'll all just leave us here."

"It's too dangerous—" Hunter began.

"I know he's a pain," I said, "but I don't sense any real danger from him."

"Morgan can take care of herself, you know," said Sky. "And it's true. Killian doesn't have that antagonistic streak with her, while I think the rest of us could cheerfully strangle him."

"All right," Hunter agreed at last. "But I'm going to be in the coffee shop in the building. If anything feels dangerous or even a little bit dodgy, I want you to send me a message immediately."

I gave Hunter my word, and five minutes later Killian and I were alone in the apartment. We sat on opposite ends of the couch, watching each other. I tried to figure out why I liked someone so obnoxious. It wasn't sexual attraction. It was something else, something equally as strong. Despite his being clearly amoral and self-centered, there was something oddly lovable about Killian. Maybe it was that he genuinely seemed to like me.

"Are you all right?" he asked. The gentleness in his voice took me by surprise.

"Why wouldn't I be?"

"I don't know," Killian said. "I don't know you very well, do I? But I sense you're feeling weaker than you're used to. Drained, maybe."

Be wary of him, I told myself. "I'm just tired," I said.

"Right, it's been a long day." He glanced at the green stuff sack on the floor. "I could turn in, I suppose, behave myself and make the Seeker happy."

"He's just trying to protect you," I said.

Anger flickered in Killian's dark eyes. "I never asked for protection."

"You need it," I said. "Your own father is trying to kill you."

Killian waved his hand. "The Seeker was going on about the same thing. Let me tell you, right? It's not likely my dad would go after me. He's got much bigger fish to fry, as the saying goes." Killian looked over his shoulder at the kitchen. "Now, there's one thing the States is lacking, a good fish-and-chips joint. I could use some right now, in fact."

"You're out of luck," I said testily. "Back to the subject. Your father is the leader of Amyranth?"

Killian got up and walked over to the window. He leaned his palms against the sill and stared out into the darkness. "My dad is a very powerful witch. I respect his power. I'd be a bloody madman not to. I stay out of his way. He's got no reason to want me dead."

He hadn't answered the question, I noticed with interest. "What about your mother?" I asked.

Killian laughed mirthlessly and turned to face me. "Grania? The bird's got generations of magick in her blood, but does she appreciate it? Not at all. She gets her real power from being a victim. No matter what happens, she suffers. Nobly, dramatically, and loudly. I tell you, I completely understand why my dad left that house. I couldn't wait to get out myself."

"So you came to New York to be with him?" I asked.

"No," he said. "I knew he was here, of course. And there were certain . . . connections for me in the city because of him. But Dad's a heartless bastard. We're not what you would call close." He polished off his soda and looked at me. "What about you? What's your story?"

I shrugged, not wanting to lie about myself, but knowing I shouldn't tell him anything of my real story.

"You're a blood witch," he stated.

I nodded. That much I couldn't hide from him.

"Quite powerful, I can sense that," he went on. "And for reasons that are unfathomable to me, you're quite fond of that bore of a Seeker."

"That's enough," I said sharply.

Killian laughed. "Right. Didn't take me long to find your sore point, did it?"

"Are you always this much fun?" I asked, irritated.

Killian put his hand over his heart and looked to the ceiling. "May the gods strike me dead," he said with mock solemnity. "Always."

"If you weren't running from your father, then who were you running from?" I asked, unable to give it up. "And don't tell me you weren't running."

He looked at me again. All of a sudden the mirth went out of his eyes. "All right," he said, leaning forward. "It's like this. I don't really believe the Seeker is right about me being an Amyranth target," he went on in a hushed voice. "On the other hand, it is true that Amyranth isn't exactly pleased with me. See, I'd all but joined the coven. Never went through with the initiation, but I was in deep enough to learn some of their secrets, the minor ones at least. Then I . . . decided that I didn't want to join. But Amyranth isn't the sort of coven you just walk out on. And my dad took the defection a bit personally."

"It sounds like it took courage to defect," I said, genuinely starting to like him. "What made you do it?"

Killian gave another of his casual shrugs. "I just wasn't into their whole agenda."

"Why not?" Finally, I thought, we were getting somewhere.

But he just winked at me. "Too much homework," he said with a laugh. "Took up all my quality time. New York is a blast. Don't you think it's kind of a waste to spend all your time feeling like one of the witches in a bad production of *Macbeth*?"

I couldn't tell anymore if Killian was being honest or just playing with me. "I think—"

I never finished my sentence because suddenly my witch

senses were on red alert, shrieking in alarm. Killian felt it, too. He was on his feet in an instant, his gaze sweeping the apartment.

"What the hell is that?" I whispered. The sense of menace was so sharp, it was almost physical.

"Someone's trying to get into the apartment," he said.

Instantly I sent a message to Hunter. Then I ran to the video monitor in the hall and pressed the button for the doorman. "Did anyone come past you?" I asked him, trying to keep my voice normal. "Did you send anyone up to this apartment?"

"Bollocks to that," Killian muttered. He peered through the peephole in the door and did a scan of the hallway. "No one there," he reported a moment later. His face was pale. "But someone is definitely paying attention to us. Someone unfriendly."

Something thumped hard against the living room window, and I jumped about a foot in the air. Killian and I both spun around. I got a brief impression of feathers in motion.

"Oh, thank God!" I said, weak with relief. "It was only a pigeon. I thought someone was trying to climb in the window."

The front door flew open, and Hunter burst in. "What is it?" he asked breathlessly.

I ran to him. "Someone's out there," I said, resisting the urge to bury my face in his chest. "Someone's watching us."

"What?" His eyes widened. "Tell me what happened."

My words tumbled over one another as I told him how Killian and I had both felt the hostile attention, how we'd been unable to pin down where it was coming from or who it was. Killian didn't say anything, just nodded every now and then. His face was still pale, but I figured that was normal, after what we'd sensed.

Looking grim, Hunter began to prowl through the apartment. I could tell that his senses were fully extended, and I felt something else besides—probably some Seeker spell he was using to get the danger to reveal itself.

"Nothing," he said, walking back into the living room. "Which doesn't mean that there wasn't something very real trying to get in. Only that whatever it was seems to be gone now." He looked at Killian. "Anything else you noticed that might help us?"

Killian shook his head. "No. Nothing," he said, sounding almost angry. Then he added abruptly, "Look, I'm knackered. I'm going to sleep." Ignoring the air mattress, he stretched out on the couch and rolled over, presenting his back to us.

A moment later the door opened again and the rest of our group came into the apartment. Apparently they had gone to some club where a terrible band was playing and everyone else was in their fifties. There was a good deal of loud discussion of just whose bad idea it had been. Throughout it Killian lay on the couch, eyes closed. He seemed to be asleep, though I didn't see how it was really possible, given the noise level in the room.

After a few moments I retreated to the guest room and crawled into bed. It had been a long day, and in spite of everything on my mind, I fell asleep quickly.

When I woke just before ten the next morning, Hunter was cursing.

Killian was gone.

9

Connections

November 11, 1981

I thought it would get easier. Isn't time supposed to heal all wounds? And if not time, what about the healing rituals our clan has used for hundreds of years?

Why is it that I see Maeve's face when I wake and when I sleep and when I lie in bed with Grania? Maeve, behind every door, around every corner, in every invocation to the Goddess? There is no longer any joy for me in this world. Even my own children cannot hold my interest or attention, and that's probably a kindness. If I really let myself see them, I see them as the things that made Maeve reject me. If not for them, she and I would be together now. I can't forget her. And I can't have her. And the rage does not ebb.

It's funny. Fat, old Greer, of all people, was the one who saw what was happening. She didn't mince words. "Your soul is sickening and your heart shriveling," she told me. "There's a black, twisted thing inside you. So use it, boy."

At first I was so out of my mind with pain, I didn't understand what she meant. It was not hard to figure out, though. Who better to call on dark magick than one whose own soul has sunk into darkness?

—Neimhidh

Hunter was staring out the living room window at a leaden winter sky, his jaw tight with frustration. Raven was still sleeping, and Robbie had gone out to get bagels.

Bree sat cross-legged on the living room floor, doing a yoga stretch. "Look, I know you're trying to protect Killian, but personally, I'm not sure his being gone is such a loss."

From the couch Sky said, "I know what you mean."

Hunter's eyes focused on me. "I want to go over what happened last night when you and Killian sensed that hostile presence. I know you think you told me everything, but tell me again. Even the littlest details, no matter how unimportant they might seem."

I sat down on the couch. "We were in the living room, just talking, when we both felt a presence. Killian said something was trying to get into the apartment. I sent that message to you then, and we both searched with our senses. Then I went to the intercom and called the doorman to see if he'd seen anyone. Killian did a scan of the hallway. And then there was a big thump at the window that nearly scared us both to death—"

"You didn't mention anything about a thump last night," Hunter said sharply.

"That's because was it nothing. Just a pigeon. And then right after that you showed up."

Hunter frowned. "A pigeon?"

"What?" I said. "What's wrong?"

"Pigeons aren't nocturnal," Hunter said. He looked tense. "What exactly did you see?"

I felt a stirring of alarm. "Um, it was just a blur. Feathers. Brown and gray, I think. About this big." I held up my hands to make a shape the size of a large cantaloupe.

"That's too big to be a pigeon," Hunter said instantly. "I suspect it was an owl."

My mouth went dry. "You mean . . ."

He nodded. "I mean one of the shape-shifters from Amyranth."

There was a long silence. I tried to still the flutterings of terror in my stomach.

"At least we can be reasonably sure we were right about Killian being their target," Hunter said. "Obviously Amyranth followed him here."

"He knew," I said, suddenly understanding why Killian was so subdued after the "pigeon" incident. "He didn't tell us, but I'm sure he knew exactly what it was."

Hunter blew out a long breath. "Now the question is whether Killian cut out on his own or whether Amyranth somehow managed to spirit him away. But it all comes down to the same thing. Somehow we've got to find him before anything happens to him."

I thought about Ciaran's watch, wondering if we could

somehow use it to figure out where Ciaran was. "Hunter," I said, feeling nervous. "I need to show you something. Come with me for a minute."

Bree and Sky both gave me questioning looks as Hunter followed me into the guest room. Wishing I'd been straight with him from the start, I took the watch from my jacket pocket and handed it to him.

One blond eyebrow arched as he unwrapped the green silk covering. "Where did you get this?" he asked, his eyes unreadable.

I told him the whole story then.

Hunter listened silently. Then for an endless stretch he just looked at me. I didn't need my witch senses to know that I'd disappointed him—by acting so rashly, by having kept the whole thing secret from him, especially once I knew Ciaran was the Amyranth leader.

"I'm sorry," I said. "I should have told you."

"Yes. You should have." He sounded weary. "Nevertheless, the watch might be a valuable aid. Let's see if it will help us." He wound the stem a few turns. "Since you're connected to Maeve and it was hers, you need to be the one to hold it."

I took the watch from him and held it in my hand. Intuitively we both slipped into a meditative state, focusing on the rhythm of the watch's ticking.

Hunter chanted a few words in Gaelic. "A spell to make visible the energies of those who once held the watch dear," he explained.

I felt a warmth along the watch's golden case and a rush of tenderness wound through with what I'd come to recognize as my mother's energy.

"Maeve cherished it," I told Hunter.

He sketched a rune in the air, and I recognized Peorth, the rune for hidden things revealed. "What else?" he asked.

Something flickered along the surface of the shiny, gold case. A bit of green. Maeve's wide green eyes, then her russet-colored hair. I felt my throat go thick with tears. The last time I'd seen a vision of Maeve, it had been of her trapped in the burning barn. Dying.

Here she stood in an open field, her eyes lit with joy and love. The image changed. This time it showed Maeve in what must have been her bedroom. A small space tucked under the eaves with a narrow bed covered by a brightly colored quilt. Maeve stood in a white nightgown, gazing from her window at the moon, a look of yearning on her face. I was sure she was thinking about Ciaran.

Now show me Ciaran, I entreated the watch silently. But there was only Maeve, and her image lasted just a moment before fading away.

I looked up at Hunter. "Not much help, I'm afraid. Just my mother from back before I was born."

"Are you okay?" he asked.

I nodded, wrapped the watch back in its green silk, and returned it to my jacket pocket.

"Well, there's one more thing I can try," Hunter said. He reached into his back pocket and drew out what looked like a playing card, only on it was an image of the Virgin Mary, shown with a spiky golden halo and a little angel over her head.

"The Virgin of Guadalupe," Hunter explained. "When I finally found Killian in the abandoned building last night,

I found this in there with him. I've traced it to its source."

"Huh?" I wasn't following this at all.

Hunter smiled. "Want to come with me and see where he got it?"

My day suddenly looked brighter. I was going to spend it with Hunter!

In the living room we had a brief confab about plans for the day. Sky and Raven were going to the Cloisters. Bree and Robbie were still undecided. We were all going to meet that night for our one real restaurant splurge.

Hunter and I walked across town to the West Village. Hunter led the way to a small store just west of Hudson Street. The shop's crowded window was filled with candles in colored glass jars, crosses, rosaries, statues of the saints, gazing crystals, herbs, oils, and powders. We stepped inside, and I smelled an odd blend: frankincense and rosemary, musk and myrrh.

"This is weird," I whispered to Hunter. "It feels like a cross between an outlet for church goods and a Wiccan store."

"The woman who runs this place is a *curandera*," Hunter explained in a low voice. "A Mexican white witch. Central American witchcraft often has a good deal of Christian symbolism mixed in with the Wicca." He rang a bell on the counter. My eyes widened as a beautiful, dark-haired woman stepped out from the back room. It was the witch from the club, the one who'd told me that I needed to heal my own heart.

"*Buenos días,*" she said. Her eyes lingered on me, and there was a silent moment in which we each recognized and acknowledged each other. "Can I help you?"

Hunter held out the card with the Virgin on it. "Is this from your shop?"

She studied it for a moment, then gazed up at him. "*Sí.* I sometimes give these cards to those in need of protection. How did you trace it to me?"

"It carries the pattern of your energy."

"Most witches wouldn't be able to pick that up," she said. "I put spells on my cards so that they can't be traced." She looked at him more carefully. "You're from the council?"

He nodded. "I'm looking for a witch called Killian. I think he's in danger."

"That one is always in danger," she said, but her eyes were suddenly wary.

"Do you know where he is?" Hunter asked.

Silently she shook her head.

"If you see him," Hunter said, "would you contact me?"

She gazed at him again, and I had the feeling that she was reading him the way she'd read me. "Yes," she said at last, "I will."

Hunter hesitated, then said, "Do you know anything about Amyranth?"

"*Brujas!*" she said, shivering. "They worship darkness. You don't want to go near them."

"We think they may have Killian," Hunter said.

Something unreadable flickered in her eyes. Then she scrawled a name on a piece of paper and handed it to Hunter. "She once had the misfortune to be the lover of Amyranth's leader. She has been trapped in terror ever since. I don't know if she'll talk to you, but you can try. Show her my card."

"Thank you," Hunter said. We turned to go.

"There's something you've been putting off, Seeker," the woman said.

Hunter turned back to face her, startled. "Do it now," she urged him. "Do not hesitate. Otherwise you may be too late. *Comprende?*"

I was baffled, but Hunter's eyes widened. "Yes," he said slowly.

"Wait, I have something that might help you." The woman disappeared into the back room and reappeared with what looked like a large seedpod. "You know what to do with this?" she asked.

"Yes," Hunter said again. His face had turned pale. "Thank you."

"*Hasta luego, chica,*" she called to me as we left.

"What was that all about?" I asked when we were outside.

Hunter took my arm and steered me west, toward the Hudson River. "She's befriended Killian," he explained. "She's been trying to help him. I'm fairly certain she's the one who told him to hide out in that building in Chelsea. The church across the street was called Our Lady of Guadalupe."

"But what was she talking about at the end?"

He was silent for almost a block. Then he said, "She's very empathic. She can pick up on people's deep fears and worries."

"I noticed," I said, thinking back to what she'd said to me at the club. "And?"

"And . . . she picked up on my worry about my mum and dad. She gave me a safe way to contact them—I think. With this." He stared at the seedpod.

"How does it work?" I asked.

"Indirectly, as I understand it," Hunter said. "I've never used one of these before—they're rather a specialty of Latin witches. It's supposed to work something like a message in a bottle, but with a very low-level finding spell on it that will seek out the person you're trying to reach. The spell is so slight that with any luck, it will slip right under the radar of anyone who might be watching. The drawback is that with such a weak spell, the message could take a while to reach its destination—and anything might happen to it along the way." He sucked in a deep breath. "But I have to try it."

"Are you sure you should?" I asked hesitantly. "I mean, the council told you to leave it to them. I know I'm not the council's biggest fan in general, but maybe they're right about this. It seems too dangerous for you to do on your own."

"They've had no success," Hunter said. "And I've been getting the feeling that time is short—that I've got to contact Mum and Dad now. I hope I'm wrong, but I don't dare wait any longer and find out too late that I was right."

The wind rose as we drew closer to the river. "This way," Hunter said, leading me to a small commercial pier. There was a metal gate with a lock on the pier, but Hunter spelled it, and it popped open. We walked through the gate and past a bunch of industrial drums and crates.

Hunter knelt by the water, a smooth sheet of lead gray. Carefully he opened the pod. I watched as he drew sigils that glittered softly on the air before disappearing into the pod. He sang a long Gaelic chant, something unknown to me. Then he closed the pod and wrapped it in more spells. Finally he threw the pod into the water. We watched it bob on the surface for a few moments. I gasped as it finally sank beneath a swell.

Hunter reached out and took my hand, and I tried to give him my strength. "I've done what I can," he said. "Now I just have to wait—and hope."

10

Signs

December 14, 1981

Greer has been dead a month now of a heart attack, and if anyone suspects that I helped to hasten her death, they dare not accuse me. Liathach is mine now. Andarra, Grania's father, doesn't quite understand that. He's still grieving. He came to tonight's circle and chanted the opening invocation to the Goddess and the God. His eyes filled with confusion when I thanked him for it and took over. I had to. He wanted to spend the entire night sending on Greer's soul, which I believe we took care of immediately after her death. She had so many dealings with the taibhs, the dark spirits. Doesn't he know they came for her in the end?

It's almost Yule, the time of the return of the God, an appropriate time for me to take over Liathach. Greer was *a power, I'll grant, but she wasn't bold enough. She was always worrying about the council. It's time to turn the tables. Now Liathach will come into its own, and the council will fear us.*

—Neimhidh

Hunter came back to the apartment with me, then went off to look for Ciaran's former lover. Bree had gone for a pedicure, and Robbie and I were alone in the apartment. I was glad—I wanted to try to work things out with him. But to my dismay, when I came back into the living room after using the bathroom, he was pulling on his coat.

"Where are you going?" I asked, feeling forlorn.

"Museum of Natural History," Robbie said briefly. He'd barely spoken to me since our argument.

"Want company?"

"Not really."

"Okay," I said, trying not to show how much that hurt. "But Robbie? I've been thinking a lot about what you said yesterday. I need to talk to you about it. Um—can I walk you to the subway?"

After a moment he nodded, and I put my coat back on. We walked up to Twenty-third Street. Robbie's plan was to take the bus across to Eighth Avenue, where he could pick up the C train. The wide cross street was jammed with buses, trucks, and taxis. An ambulance and a fire truck, sirens wailing, tried to make their way through the gridlock. Talking—or rather, hearing—was almost impossible.

"Want to stop in a coffee shop?" I shouted over the commotion. "My treat."

"Not really," Robbie said again. He stepped forward as a bus pulled up to the stop.

I gritted my teeth. "Okay," I said. "We'll talk on the bus."

Fortunately the bus wasn't too crowded. We got a seat together. "I want to apologize to you," I said. "You were right—I shouldn't have messed with that woman."

Robbie looked straight ahead. He was still angry.

"This being a blood witch and having power, it's still kind of new to me," I went on. "I'm not saying that excuses what I did. Only that I'm still getting used to it, still trying to figure out when I should and shouldn't use magick. And the truth is, the power is a kick. I get tempted to use it when I shouldn't. So I'm probably going to screw up now and then."

Robbie folded his arms across his chest. "Tell me something I don't know."

I sighed. "You're not making this easy."

He looked at me coldly. "You can make it easy. Just cast a spell on me."

I winced. "Robbie, listen. I promise I'll be more careful. I give you my word that I'm going to be more conscious and try not to abuse my power. And I'll never put you in a bad position again."

Robbie shut his eyes. When he opened them, the anger was gone and in its place was sorrow. "Morgan, I'm not trying to punish you. I just don't know how to trust you anymore," he said. "I don't know how we can be friends. I don't want to lose you, but—" He raised his hands in a gesture of helplessness. "You've got all the power. The playing field is nowhere near level. That makes it pretty hard to have a real friendship."

I felt my hope draining away. I'd assumed that we would talk and everything would be okay again. Robbie and I had never stayed angry with each other before. But Robbie was right. Things were unequal. I was operating in a different realm now, with different rules.

He got off the bus, and I followed him down the steps into the subway station. The train came, and we got on it.

"So, my being a blood witch means I've got to lose your friendship?" I bit down on my lip to keep from crying as the train moved out of the station.

"I don't know," Robbie said. "I don't know what to do about it."

We hurtled through several stops, during which I did my best not to break into tears. Things with Bree would never be the same. And now I was losing Robbie, too. Why did being a blood witch mean I had to give up my best friends?

The subway came to a stop at Seventy-second Street, and I glanced at the map. The next stop was Robbie's.

"I don't want to give up on our friendship," I said stubbornly. "I need you. I need Robbie who's not a blood witch and who knows me better than almost anyone. I—" I wiped my nose. "Robbie, you're one of the best people I've ever met. I can't bear to lose you."

Robbie gave me a long, complicated look—sympathy, love, and a weary exasperation all bound together. "I don't want to give up on us, either," he said just as the subway rolled into the Eighty-first Street station. "You want to come see some dinosaurs?"

"Sure." I managed a shaky smile.

We got off the train together, but as we walked through

the turnstiles, a cloud of intense exhaustion dropped down over me. Then came vague nausea.

"Uh . . . Robbie? I think I need to bail on the museum."

"After all that? You won't even see dinosaurs with me?"

"I want to, but I feel really wrung out all of a sudden. I think I just need to sit down for a while."

"You sure?" he asked.

I nodded. I wanted to give Robbie a hug, but by this time I was focusing on not throwing up. He hovered uncertainly for a moment. Then he said, "Okay. See you later," and walked toward the museum.

I crossed the street to the park and sat down on one of the benches. The nausea hadn't let up. If anything, I felt worse, weak and disoriented. I shut my eyes for a second.

When I opened them again, I was no longer looking at the wide steps and columns of the museum. The scene in front of me had changed.

A blur of gray-brown branches. Across from them, a tall, narrow house obscured by snaky, tangled wisteria vines. Sirens and an emergency light flashing, cars speeding by. A doorbell hidden in a stone gorgon's head. Screams and the sound of a struggle. A man's voice, familiar but somehow terrifying. Blurry figures wearing animal masks. A bound figure, lying on a stone table.

I felt something nudging my ankle, and I snapped out of the vision with a cry, startling the poor dog who was sniffing my shoe. The dog's owner pulled it away, giving me an indignant look.

Goddess, what was that? I wondered. I'd never had anything like it before—a waking vision, something that just came to me with no prompting. It was clearly connected to the dream I'd had. But it was different—more real somehow. Was I seeing Killian being tortured by Amyranth?

I had to talk to Hunter. I sent him an urgent witch message. Then I sat there, shaken, waiting for him to answer. But there was no response. Hunter, now is not the time to ignore me, I thought. I tried again, letting my fear permeate the message.

Still nothing. I felt a flicker of fear. It wasn't like him to ignore an urgent summons. Had something happened to him? After waiting another minute I tried Sky. But she didn't respond, either. Were my messages even getting through?

Trying not to give in to panic, I found a pay phone and pulled out the phone card my parents had given me for emergencies. I punched in the number of the apartment. No one answered, but I left a message just in case Hunter or Sky came in.

Next I called Bree's cell phone. Bree picked up at once. "Speak," she said loftily.

"It's me," I said. "Where are you?"

"In a cab, stuck in traffic." She sounded irked.

"Bree," I said, "I think I saw Killian."

"What? Where?"

I told Bree about the vision I'd just had. "I'm sure Ciaran's got him, only I can't figure out where they are. I've got to find that house," I finished. I thought of how Hunter had used what we'd seen when I'd scryed to find Killian. Maybe Bree and I could do the same thing. "I need your help."

"Okay." Bree sounded hesitant. "Um—what can I do?"

"You know the city better than I do," I said. "Think about

what I described and help me figure out where it might be."

"Oh, I get it. Cool idea," she said. "Um—okay, you say you saw a blur of branches?"

When I said yes, Bree said, "It sounds like this house you saw was by a park. Maybe Central Park."

"Right. Makes sense," I said, feeling a flicker of excitement.

"Okay, now, where, exactly, were the trees?"

I closed my eyes and tried to call up the vision. "I was standing on a corner. The house was across a narrow street from me, and the blur was in my right eye. I think the trees were across a wide street from the house. Yeah, the house was on a corner. The front door faced a side street. . . . At the corner there was a wide avenue, and the trees were on the other side."

"Now we're getting somewhere. Okay, let's think. . . . Describe the avenue. How wide was it? And which way was the traffic going?" Bree pressed.

"Jesus, Bree," I said, frustrated. "I wasn't paying attention to traffic patterns."

"Think," she insisted over the blare of horns. "Could you see any cars at all?"

I forced my mind back to the siren and the flashing emergency light. The light was on top of an ambulance. I followed it in my mind until a blue SUV passed on its left. . . . "It was at least four lanes wide, and the cars were going both ways," I said. "It was two-way traffic. Hey!" I knew most of the avenues were one way. That narrowed it down a lot.

Bree's voice rose with excitement. "It sounds like the house is somewhere on Central Park West. Two-way traffic . . . a wide avenue with a park on one side . . . a fancy house . . . I can't think of anyplace else in Manhattan that looks like that."

"Bree, you're brilliant," I said fervently.

"Where are you now?" she asked.

"Right by the Museum of Natural History."

"Perfect," Bree said. "Why don't you just walk along Central Park West and see if you can find anything that looks familiar?"

Bree was right—it was perfect. I might be within a few blocks of the house right now. I might actually find Killian—and Ciaran. I felt my chest constrict with fear.

"Morgan? Are you there?" Bree asked.

"I'm here," I said. "Listen, I'm going to look for this place. Can you try to track down Hunter? Tell him I need him now!"

Bree hesitated a moment. "Morgan, promise me that if you find it, you won't go in there by yourself."

"I'm not planning on it," I said, feeling a rush of warmth at her concern. "Bree—thanks for your help."

I hung up and made one more call, this one to Robbie's cell. After all, he was somewhere just across the street. But all I got was his voice mail. Robbie had turned off his phone, and I didn't have time to search the museum for him.

I tried Hunter one more time. Still nothing. Was he okay? I just had to trust that he was. And I had to trust in the fact that there were no coincidences. Fate was guiding me. I took the fact that I was on Central Park West as a sign. I was being guided to find Killian.

Focusing my eyes straight ahead, I saw the park in my peripheral vision. The blur of branches in my right eye was very much like what I'd seen in the vision.

I started walking north, and my senses began tingling.

They were charged the way the air is charged before a summer rainstorm. Everything was about to break wide open. I passed a vendor selling hot roasted chestnuts, a dog walker with half a dozen yapping dogs pulling him along. The winter wind was at my back, sweeping up Central Park West, propelling me. A sense of urgency was building; adrenaline was coursing through my veins.

At the corner of Eighty-seventh and Central Park West, I stumbled to a sudden stop, my heart hammering. There it was.

The house had four stories, and I could glimpse granite facing behind a tangle of thick, gnarled wisteria vines. Three stone steps led to the front door, where a doorbell was embedded in a stone carving of a gorgon's head. It was exactly what I'd seen in the vision.

A thin, icy cloak of fear settled around me. I was standing in front of the place where Amyranth held Killian.

11

Fated

Samhain, 1983

The rumors are true. She lives. Ballynigel was razed to the ground by the dark wave, yet Maeve Riordan and that fawning blue-eyed half-wit, Angus Bramson, managed to survive. Goddess, I've lost track of the number of times I've wished them both dead and in everlasting torment. Especially her. In the space of two enchanted weeks she opened my heart and destroyed my entire life. My marriage became a hollow sham, my home a prison. Grania hates me. The children . . . well, they respect my power, at least.

I'm leaving Scotland, leaving Liathach. The coven has grown in strength and magick as never before. We took part in the destruction of Crossbrig, which gained Liathach their much coveted Wyndenkell spell books. But the Liathach witches are *weak, fearful. They've been ruled too long by Grania's family. They think I've led them into danger. They want to retreat. Well, let them. But I won't be a part of it.*

I don't care about leaving Liathach. I should have done it years ago. All that matters is that I find Maeve. She has done the impossible. She survived the dark wave. I've scryed, and I've seen her. I know that she still holds me in her heart, that we are still meant to be together. I can't live without her another day. Now I must find her.

The only question is whether it will be to tell her how much I love her . . . or to kill her.

—Neimhidh

The house was old, a part of the city left over from the nineteenth century. The worn stonework had a faded elegance, and the thick tangle of wisteria vines reminded me of the Briar Rose fairy tale. A sleeping princess hidden behind a wall of thorns . . . But Killian was no fictional princess, and I was no rescuer prince. Now that I'd found it, what on earth was I going to do?

I crossed the street to another pay phone and called Bree again. She'd just gotten back to the apartment.

"I found it," I told her. "It's right on the corner of Central Park West and Eighty-seventh. Have you heard anything from Hunter?"

"Nada," Bree answered. "Any idea where he might be?"

Nothing immediately jumped to mind. Hunter was always so careful and secretive about his work. He told me only what he thought I needed to know.

"Um . . . there's a Mexican witch's shop he took me to off Hudson Street. She's the one who told him about the woman he's searching for. She might give you the address."

"I'll find her," Bree promised. "But first I'll leave a note here in case he comes back."

"I'm going to stay here and keep an eye on the house," I told Bree. "If you find Hunter, will you tell him to meet me here?"

"Okay. But call me again in twenty minutes," Bree ordered. "I want to know that you're safe."

I promised I would. Then I sat down on one of the park benches that offered a clear view of the house. It was not a day for sitting outside. The air was damp and bitter cold. Within a few minutes I could hardly feel my feet.

But I could feel the house. Even though I was across the street from it, I could sense powerful magick wrapped around it.

I thought I saw a flicker of movement in one of the upper windows, and a knot of dread lodged itself in the middle of my chest. I wished I could go off searching with Bree, I really did. The idea of staying here on my own across from this house that practically oozed evil terrified me—especially knowing that Ciaran might be inside.

I hunkered down in the cold, concentrating on the house. No one came in or out. Nothing more moved in the windows. Even the wisteria branches barely moved in the icy wind. There was a bleak stillness about the house that suddenly made me wonder if I was wrong and the place was completely deserted. Magick can fool most people, I reminded myself. But not me.

I extended my senses to see what sort of magickal

defenses or traps there might be. I picked up resistance at the door, a warding spell of some sort, but it didn't feel very serious. The house wasn't nearly as heavily spelled as Cal and Selene's house had been. I couldn't sense any electronic security systems, either, just the requisite New York combination of heavy-duty locks on the door. Only one of those bolts was actually shut. Strange.

I glanced at my watch. It was nearly three o'clock. I wondered if Bree was having any luck finding Hunter. Was there some way I could find out what was going on in the house at that very moment? I could search for Killian's aura.

I concentrated, trying to remember what it had been like. A pattern traced itself in my mind's eye so clearly that I could almost hear Killian's voice. And then what I was hearing were cries. I felt the struggle again, the helplessness, the overwhelming sense of terror and despair.

The vision was gone as quickly as it had come, but I knew what it meant. Killian was in the house, captive yet reaching out, crying for help. Maybe he wasn't calling to me specifically, but I had an awful feeling I was the only one who had heard him.

I couldn't wait for Hunter to show up. "Hang on, Killian," I muttered. "I'm coming."

I stood up and immediately began to tremble. Who was I kidding? I was a seventeen-year-old witch with all of two and a half months' experience in my craft. And I was about to go up against a coven of evil Woodbanes and the witch who'd killed Maeve and Angus? Maeve and Angus had been trained in Wicca from the day they were born. If they hadn't been able to stop Ciaran . . . The odds were beyond insane. Ciaran had killed Maeve, his *mùirn beatha dàn*. What would he do to me, her daughter?

Yet I couldn't discount the dreams and visions. I was sure I'd had them for a reason. I could almost hear Hunter reminding me that according to Wicca, nothing is random. Everything has a purpose. I wouldn't have been given those visions if I hadn't been meant do something about them. Even the fact that the school boiler had burst now seemed part of some inevitable plan. I was here in New York City because it was my fate to save Killian.

"Goddess, help me," I murmured. I drew in deep breaths, calming and grounding myself. I had all of Alyce's knowledge and more raw power than most blood witches ever encounter. I was strong, stronger than I'd been three weeks ago when Hunter and I had fought Selene and defeated her. If Ciaran was in that building, didn't I owe it to Maeve to try to stop him once and for all?

I can do this, I told myself. I was meant to do this.

I walked up to the house and stepped onto the first of the three stone steps—and stopped as a feeling of dread snaked around my insides and whispered in my mind, *Turn away. Come no farther. Go back.*

I tried to step onto the second step, but I couldn't. Terror immobilized me, the feeling that taking that one step would seal my doom.

It's a repelling spell, I told myself. It's designed to keep you out. But there's nothing really behind it. I willed the spell to show itself to me. There was a moment of resistance before I saw a glimmering on the winter air. The rune Is—the rune of obstacles, of things frozen and delayed—repeated again and again, like a series of crystalline icicles. I visualized the warmth of fire melting the runes of the warding spell, and within seconds I felt their power weaken.

The spell snapped, and I reached the top step. I found another spell on the door itself. I felt a surge of exhilaration as I realized I knew exactly what to do. It seemed so clear. Either the binding spells weren't all that complicated, or I was stronger than I realized.

This time I drew power up from the earth, from the roots of the wisteria, from the bedrock below. I gathered all the energy poured into the city streets by the myriad inhabitants of New York City. A boisterous, defiant power swelled inside me. I let it build, then flung it at the spell that guarded the door. The spell shattered. The one bolt that had been shut on the other side of the door shot open. And I stepped into the house, nearly surfing on the wave of my own magick.

I stood in a high-ceilinged foyer. The floor was inlaid marble, patterned in black and gray. A staircase led to the upper floors. I sent a witch message to Killian. Where are you? Lead me.

The next instant I was flat on my back, hit with a binding spell stronger than anything I'd ever experienced. It forced my arms flat against my sides, clamped my legs together, pressed down on my throat so I couldn't utter a sound, compressed my chest so that I fought for every breath. Oh, Goddess. Maybe I wasn't as strong as I'd thought.

Quickly I cast a spell to loosen all bindings.

It did nothing. My mind reeled in panic.

I tried the spell that had worked so brilliantly just a few minutes ago. I extended my senses out and down, searching for a connection with the ground beneath me. The hollow echo that came back was mystifying. It was as if the earth itself was empty, flat, drained of anything to give. And I was left in a place where waves of dark magick swirled around me.

Alyce, I thought. Surely Alyce knew something that would help. A spell came to me then for bringing light in the midst of darkness. I began to visualize a single white flame, growing brighter, hotter, blazing through all the dark energy, consuming it, purifying the space around me.

I almost blacked out as something that felt like a blade of jagged ice plunged into my stomach. It's an illusion, I told myself, remembering how Selene had attacked me with pain. I willed myself to go beyond it, to keep picturing the flame devouring the darkness.

Another blade drove into my back. "Aaagh!" My own strangled cry panicked me. I felt the icy blade cut through skin, muscle, bone, and the flame in my mind guttered out.

As if to reward me for losing the spell, the pain stopped.

I glanced down at my body. There were no bloody knife wounds. They had been an illusion. But the binding was real. I couldn't move. I glanced around me, searching for the source of the power that was holding me prisoner. There— I felt magick like a dark, oily cloud swirling across the town house's pristine floor. The magick of several witches, working together.

Nausea rose in the back of my throat. I was completely overpowered. What had I done? How could I have been naive and stupid enough to believe I could go up against an entire coven of Woodbanes? The second I'd walked into the house, I'd walked into their trap.

A slight figure in a black robe and a mask walked toward me. The mask showed a jackal's face, carved out of some sort of dark wood and horribly exaggerated, with an enormous snarling mouth. My fear ratcheted up another notch. Other masked figures appeared: an owl, a cougar, a viper, an eagle.

"We've got her," the jackal said, in a voice so perfectly neutral, I couldn't tell if it was male or female.

"Where's Killian?" I demanded. "What have you done with him?"

"Killian?" the witch in the owl mask repeated. The voice was distinctly female. "Killian isn't here."

"But you're going to drain him of his power!" I said stupidly.

A giddy, high-pitched laugh erupted from the jackal's mouth. "Oh, no, we're not."

"We never wanted Killian," the owl said.

"You've been misled," the viper agreed, and all of them burst out laughing. The viper's narrow golden eyes glittered as it stared at me. "You're the one we're going to drain."

12

Ciaran

February 28, 1984

The beginning of spring is a time to sow the seeds of dreams for the coming year. Here in a tiny village called Meshomah Falls, I am a boy again, full of fantasies and dreams, eager to welcome the promise of spring. I found her. Today Maeve and I saw each other for the first time since I left Ballynigel. I knew in that instant that she still loved me. That nothing had changed, that it had all been worth the wait. Goddess, I see the universe every time I gaze into her eyes.

We waited until evening, for she insisted on making some excuse to poor, pathetic Angus. Then she led me out beyond the town, through a narrow band of woods, across a meadow, and up a hill to a field. "No one will see us here," she said.

"Of course not. One of us will work a spell of invisibility," I said.

That was when Maeve told me she'd given up her magick. I couldn't believe it. Ever since she left Ireland, she's led a half life, her senses shut down, a prisoner of her own terror. "You never have to fear again," I told her. Bit by bit I coaxed her open. Oh, the joy that was in her eyes as she let herself sense the seeds in the earth beneath us, the tender green shoots waiting to break the surface. Then she opened herself to the skies, the stars, the pull of the incandescent spring moon, and we gave ourselves to pleasure and to each other.

Goddess, I have finally known true joy. All the pain I have gone through, it was all worth it for this.

—Neimhidh

"You're the one we're going to drain." The words echoed in my ears, and I suddenly saw it all with sick clarity.

My dreams and visions—they had all been premonitions of what was to be my own ordeal in this house. Not Killian's. Somehow the council got that one key detail wrong when they interpreted the dream. The wolf cub on the table wasn't Killian. It was me.

Some rational part of my mind wondered why I'd appeared as a wolf cub, but before I could make sense of it, the jackal said, "You will come with us."

I stared up defiantly. "No."

The figure waved a hand over me, and I was suddenly on my feet, the bindings loosened just enough to allow me to follow like an automaton. Fury at my own traitorous body

swept through me, but I could no more resist the spell to follow than I could break the binding spell.

I followed through a parlor and a dining room, through a
kitchen to another staircase, this one leading down.

We descended the stairs into a cellar. How could I possibly escape? The cellar door would close, and terrible things
would be done to me.

The cellar was lit by a few black candles set in wall
sconces. The owl held out a robe made of a thin, shiny brown
fabric. "Take off your clothes and put this on," she said.

The robe spooked me. I flashed on an old movie where
they burned witches at the stake and made them wear robes
like this for their execution. "What's it for?" I asked.

The witch in the hawk mask drew a sign in the air, and I
doubled over again in agony.

"Do as you're told," the jackal said.

They watched me change, and I felt the dull burn of shame
over my terror as I took off my clothes and put on the robe.
Then I was forced down into a chair, and two more masked figures—a weasel and a jaguar—came into the cellar with a
steaming cup. They forced me to drink its contents. It was
some sort of hideous herb tea—I recognized henbane, valerian,
belladonna, foxglove. The smell was so revolting, I gagged with
every sip.

When I'd drained the last sickening drop, they left me. I
felt the liquid moving through me, slowing my thoughts,
deadening my reflexes. Then my body started to tremble
uncontrollably, and I was hit by a wave of dizziness. If I'd
been able to move from the chair, I'm sure I would have

fallen to the floor. The floor itself seemed to be swaying, the walls spinning. Menacing shadows crawled in the corners of my field of vision.

I took a deep breath, trying to center myself. I whispered a quick spell drawn from my Alyce memory, and after a few moments the hallucinatory shadows receded a little. The dizziness and sluggishness remained, though.

At last I heard footsteps on the stairs. The owl and weasel returned. "He's ready for you now," the owl said.

I had no doubt of who was waiting for me. Ciaran. My mother's *mùirn beatha dàn*, the one she'd loved. The one who had killed her.

The owl waved a hand over me and muttered an incantation. Again I stood and followed with jerky motions. The dizziness didn't pass, but I found I could walk through it.

We walked up to the first floor, through the kitchen, and then up the main staircase to the second floor. I was led into a wood-paneled room lit by candles. A fire glowed in the fireplace. I was shoved into another chair. The two masked witches left and shut the door.

Ciaran stood in front of the fireplace, his back to me. He wore a robe of deep purple silk with black bands on the arms. I fought down a wave of nausea. My mother's murderer.

He turned to face me, and for a disorienting moment the trembling and the nausea vanished. In their place I felt surprise and a massive sense of relief. This wasn't Ciaran. This was the man from the courtyard and the bookstore, the man with whom I'd had such an affinity, the man in whom I'd placed such an immediate trust.

The nausea returned an instant later as I realized just how badly I'd misplaced that trust. Now I could feel the darkness of his power, like a cyclone of roiling blackness.

Ciaran watched me.

"I never asked your name," I said, my voice once again my own.

"But you know it now, don't you?" he asked. His face was harsh in the firelight, his eyes unreadable dark slashes.

"Ciaran," I said quietly.

"And you are Morgan Rowlands," he replied courteously.

Oh, Goddess, how could I have been so blind? "You've been playing with me all along," I said. "You knew who I was even before we met."

"On the contrary," he said. "I only realized you were the one Selene destroyed herself over when we talked in the bookstore."

"H-how—"

"I became curious when I sensed how powerful you were. So when we got to talking about scrying, I decided to find out more about you. My scrying stone is bound to me. Even though you were the one holding it and I was on another floor altogether, it showed me what it showed you. I saw— was it your sister?—coming out of the Widow's Vale Cineplex. The name Widow's Vale rang a bell, and then when you gave me your name, that clinched it. Truthfully," he went on, "I hadn't planned on taking care of you quite so soon, but when you just put yourself in my hands like that, I couldn't pass up the opportunity, could I?"

"The owl at the window last night—?"

"Was spying on you," he confirmed. "But then, we were

already on the alert. We've been watching the Seeker ever since he came to the city. It was easy to discover what his mission was, and after that it was child's play to set the trap, feeding you the clues that would bring you to us. I gave you the vision of Killian in the candle's flame and the vision you had today. I even helped you break the warding spells on this house. My dear, you should have known you don't have that kind of ability. Not at your level." Ciaran regarded me with a rueful smile.

I'd been such a fool. Time and again he'd manipulated me. And I'd never even suspected.

"Tell me." His tone sharpened with the command. "Where's the Seeker now?"

"I don't know."

His dark eyes raked me. How, I wondered, had I ever thought him distinguished and trustworthy? All I saw in him now was the predator, waiting to devour his prey.

Ciaran steepled his fingers. "Perhaps I shouldn't have blocked the messages you tried to send," he murmured, as if thinking aloud. "Perhaps I should have made it easier for him to find you." Then he shook his head. "No, he's clever enough that he'll find you anyway."

I sagged, despairing, as I understood what Ciaran meant. If Hunter did find me, then he would be destroyed along with me.

There was a knock on the door, and the hawk witch entered the room. I watched in disbelief as she handed Maeve's pocket watch to Ciaran. "We found this in the girl's jacket."

Ciaran's face went totally blank for a moment. Then it grew pale and distorted. "Leave!" he snapped at the hawk. Then he whirled on me. "Where did you get this?" he demanded.

"You should know!" I lashed back, glad for the chance to tell the truth. "You gave it to my mother before you murdered her!"

Ciaran stared at me, his eyes wide with undisguised shock. "Your mother?"

And I realized that Selene had never told him who I was. She'd never told him I was Maeve's daughter.

He bolted from the room then. I took it for the last moment of triumph I would ever know. I'd actually shaken the leader of Amyranth. And I'd only have to pay for it with my life.

Exhaustion descended on me like a heavy cloak. I hung my head, let my eyes close, giving in to the drug they'd fed me.

That lying, manipulative wench Selene! She knew this girl was Maeve's daughter and she never told me! What other secrets did she keep from me?

Maeve's daughter! You wouldn't know it from the girl's looks. She doesn't have Maeve's delicate, pretty face, the sprinkling of freckles across her nose, the soft waves of reddish-brown hair. All she has of Maeve is her power. Though there's something about her eyes that's damnably familiar.

How did Maeve and Angus manage to spawn that one without my ever knowing? And how the bloody hell did she find out what happened at the end? Even those who knew Maeve didn't know we were mùirn beatha dàns, and no one, save Maeve and Angus, knew about how the fire started. All witnesses are dead.

Selene couldn't have told her. Selene knew nothing of what was between me and Maeve. Or . . . did she? I've never been sure just

what Selene did and didn't know. All of which raises the question:
What else is there that Selene didn't tell me about this girl?

My thoughts are heaving like the sea. There's something at the
edge of my mind, a disturbing presence on the edge of conscious-
ness. It has a truth to show me.

Damn it. What is it? What is it?

Hunter, putting the silver chains of the *braigh* on David
Redstone . . . Mary K., huddled in a corner of Selene's study, confused, frightened, and spelled . . . Cal, absorbing the cloud of darkness that Selene hurled at me . . . His beautiful golden eyes . . .

No! I started out of my stupor, shaking and grieving at the
images that kept parading in front of me. For a moment I
couldn't imagine where I was. Then memory returned. The
house with the vines. The masked witches. Ciaran.

I was now in a much larger room. My head ached, and I felt
even dizzier than before. With effort I focused my eyes on the
ceiling, on the leaves and vines and ornate plaster molding, all
horribly familiar. Black candles flickered from sconces and
from an elaborate silver candlestick atop an inlaid ebony cabinet. Black drapes covered the windows. I cast out my senses.
They were frighteningly weak, but I could still faintly detect
objects of power inside the cabinet—athames, wands, crystals, animal skulls and bones, all emanating dark magick.

I was lying on a large round table, my hands and feet
bound to it with spelled ropes. The table was made of
some sort of stone, inlaid with patterns in another stone.
Garnet, I thought. There were deep grooves in the surface of the table. The panic I'd felt in the visions returned

full blown, and for a few useless minutes I struggled against the bonds.

Panic never helps, I told myself. Focus. Find a way out of this. But it was so hard to think through the haze of Amyranth's drugged tea.

I called on the spell that was binding me to reveal itself. I saw the faintest glimmering of something that might have been a rune before it winked out. I tried to summon the spell again. Nothing happened, and I felt another jolt of panic. Breathe, I told myself, just breathe.

But it wasn't easy. What had happened to my precious magick? I couldn't connect with it, couldn't feel it.

It's mine, dammit, I thought furiously. No one—especially not Ciaran—is going to take my magick from me.

Maybe I lost consciousness again. I'm not sure. I never heard a door open or close, never heard footsteps, but suddenly Amyranth surrounded me. Witches in robes and animal masks formed a perfect circle around the table. Jackal, owl, weasel, cougar, eagle, bear, hawk, viper, jaguar, and a wolf. Predators all. The masks seemed distorted, horrible caricatures of the animals they represented, but I could also tell there was something wrong with my eyesight. It was impossible to say how accurate my perceptions were.

My visions and dreams had come together. Even through the haze of the drug, I could appreciate the irony of it all—if we hadn't tried to prevent my dream from coming to pass, none of this would have ever happened. Never try to mess with destiny.

The bear murmured an incantation, and I realized the power-draining ritual was beginning. The others picked up the incantation, turning it into a low, insistent chant. They moved widdershins. The air felt cruel and thick with danger. This was a Wiccan circle of destruction.

And Ciaran was leading it. I couldn't see his face beneath the wolf mask, but I could hear his voice, familiar yet terrifying. Just like the vision. Goddess.

I could feel Amyranth's dark magick flowing around the circle. It crackled like lightning. The air was charged with it. Slowly the strength of their power intensified. I felt an unbearable pressure along every inch of my body. Amyranth was calling up a ravenous darkness.

Irrelevantly, it hit me that Cal had never had a funeral. The council had taken his and Selene's bodies. As far as everyone in Widow's Vale was concerned, Cal and Selene had simply vanished from the earth.

Or maybe it wasn't so irrelevant. That was what was going to happen to me. My family would never know the truth about my disappearance, and it would always torment them.

The circle stopped moving. A thick, black mist clung to its members. "We give thanks," Ciaran said, "for delivering to us a sacrifice whose powers will make us that much stronger."

"How much power does she have?" asked the owl.

Ciaran shrugged. "See for yourself."

The owl held a hand over my stomach. Fine silver needles of light dropped from it. For a second they hovered inches above me, then began to glow red. The owl murmured a syllable, and the burning needles dropped down. I couldn't hold back a scream as they seemed to pierce my skin. Dozens of sharp embers sank into my belly, my arms, my legs. Involuntarily my back arched, and I pulled against the spelled ropes.

"Stop it!" I cried. "Please, stop it!"

"Be quiet!" the owl said harshly.

And then the fiery torture intensified, burned deeper into my body. I imagined my heart shriveling into a blackened lump, my bones crisping. I was wild with pain.

I can't take this, I thought frantically. I'm going to lose my mind.

"That's enough," Ciaran ordered. "You've seen what's in her."

"Strong, very strong. She'll serve well," the owl agreed.

As suddenly as it had started, the pain was gone. I sobbed in relief and hated myself for that weakness.

The wail of a siren came faintly from outside, and a flash of red light shone through the black drapes. The vision again. Oh God, every detail was coming true. I had seen the future. Now I was living it. Amyranth was going to steal my powers, leave me drained, hollowed out—without magick, without a soul, without life.

Ciaran began another chant. One by one the others joined their voices to his. Again the dark energy began to move, gaining power as it traveled through Amyranth's circle. I lay there helpless on the stone table, every muscle in my body clenched tight against the next horrible assault.

I thought of Maeve, my mother, murdered. I thought of Mackenna, my grandmother, killed when the dark wave destroyed Ballynigel. My family had suffered for their magick. Maybe no more was being asked of me than had been asked of them. I had the Riordan strength flowing through my veins. I had ancestral memories and a legacy of incredible power. Surely that meant I had their courage as well.

Give it to us. I felt the darkness clawing at me, trying to find its way into my very marrow.

Amyranth continued the chant. The dark energy shifted, no longer crackling around the circle. Now it hovered over the table, wreathing my body with sparking purple-black light.

Give it to us.

The purple-black light licked at my skin the way flames lick at dry wood. There was no pain, but I felt a crushing weight in my mind, against my chest, in my belly. I gasped for breath and could find none. But I could not let them get my power. Desperately, silently, I sang my summon-power chant.

An di allaigh an di aigh
An di allaigh an di ne ullah
An di ullah be . . .

The words that I knew from ancestral memory were suddenly gone from me. *An di ullah be . . .* I got no further. The chant had been wiped from my mind.

No! I wanted to scream, to sob, but I had no breath. Don't take it! No! Grief consumed me—grief for the magick that was being taken from me. Grief for this precious life that I was about to lose. Grief for Hunter, whom I would never see again.

Ciaran held out a silver athame. A ruby glowed dully on its hilt. He pointed the athame at me, and the dark power coagulated into a spear of searing light.

"You will give us your power," he said.

No, no, no! I was no longer capable of coherent thought. Just—no!

The chanting broke off abruptly at a sound on the other side of the door. A muffled disturbance, a struggle . . . someone using magick against Amyranth's spells.

Hunter! I felt Hunter's presence, his love, his desperate fear for me. And it terrified me more than anything. Was I strong enough still to send a witch message? Hunter, go back, I pleaded. Don't come in here. You can't save me.

The doorknob turned with a click, and Hunter stepped into the room, his eyes wild. He glanced at me quickly as if to reassure himself that I was alive, then turned to Ciaran.

"Let her go," Hunter commanded. His voice shook.

The jackal and the wolf raised their hands, as if to attack Hunter with witch light. Ciaran stopped them.

"No!" he said. "This one is mine. At least for now." He turned back to Hunter, an expression of mild amazement on his face. "The council must be in bad shape, sending a boy to do a Seeker's work. Did they really lead you to believe you could take me on?"

Hunter's hand shot out, and a ball of witch light zoomed toward Ciaran. Ciaran drew a sigil in the air, and the light reversed course and blazed back at Hunter.

Hunter ducked, his face pale, eyes glittering. When he stood again, he looked taller, broader than he had only a moment before. A new aura of power glowed around him. He emanated both youthful strength and ancient authority.

The council. Sky had once told me that when Hunter acted as a Seeker, he had access to the extraordinary powers of the council. It was a dangerous weapon to call on, taxing to the Seeker, reserved only for emergencies. Like this one.

Hunter stepped forward. The silver chains of the *braigh* glimmered in his hands. He intended to bind Ciaran, to bind his magick. But I could sense no fear in Ciaran at all.

"Hunter, don't!" I croaked. "He'll kill you!"

"This is getting tiresome," Ciaran said. He muttered a few syllables, and the *braigh* suddenly dropped from Hunter's hand. I saw him bite back a scream.

Desperately I summoned the source of all my magick. "Maeve and Mackenna of Belwicket," I whispered, "I call on your power. Help me now!"

Nothing happened. No awakening of magick. Nothing. I was sick with disbelief. My mother's and grandmother's magick had failed me.

Ciaran said, "Bind him," and the other members of the coven surrounded Hunter and enclosed him in binding spells. The jackal gave Hunter a savage kick. He went down with a groan.

"Stop it!" I cried. My voice came out as little more than a whisper.

"I'm sorry, Morgan," Hunter said, and the grief in his voice broke my heart. "I've failed you."

"No, you haven't. It's all right, love," I said, trying to comfort him. I couldn't say more. Total, soul-destroying despair overtook me. It was I who had failed him. Hunter and I were both lost now, and all because of my fatal arrogance. Neither one of us was going to get out alive. I'd signed my own death warrant and Hunter's as well.

"Put him somewhere safe," Ciaran ordered. "We'll take care of him later."

The jackal and the weasel dragged Hunter out of the room. A few moments later they returned. The bear picked up the chant again. The ritual was resuming. I didn't care.

The animals circled widdershins. The circle suddenly stopped moving and parted. And Ciaran in his wolf mask stepped to the head of the table. He placed a deliberate hand on either side of my forehead.

"No!" I screamed. I knew what was going to happen. He was going to force *tàth meànma* on me. Even if I hadn't been drugged and weak, I doubted I would have stood a chance against Ciaran. He was the strongest witch I'd ever known. He'd have access to my every memory, thought, and dream. There was nothing I could hide from him.

I tried to sink into the haze that was clouding my mind. I tried to have no thought. I felt Ciaran's power streaming through his hands into me. For a heartbeat I fought him, and then I was hallucinating, reliving my life in flashes from the moment of my birth. Watching and feeling image after image as they flared in bright, almost unnatural colors.

The rush of air, light, and sound as I came through the darkness of the birth canal.

Angus, with his fair hair and bright blue eyes, touching my arm, tentative and sweet.

A day later. Maeve cradling me, gazing into my face with tears running down her cheeks. Saying, "You have your father's eyes."

"Bloody hell!" It was Ciaran swearing.

He broke the connection, and my vision clouded over. Another spell to obscure something they didn't want me to see. I heard footsteps and the sound of a door closing.

The air in the room had changed. Ciaran was gone. And so was Hunter.

13

Truth

February 29, 1984

The light of day dawns . . . and with it love dies.

Maeve woke in my arms. Morning dew glistened on her skin. I pulled a bit of straw from her hair and told her how beautiful she was.

"No, Ciaran!" She scrambled to her feet. "This can't be. I've made my life with Angus, and you have a wife and children—"

"Forget my wife and children. I've left them. And damn Angus!" I cried. "I'm tired of things coming between what we know is meant to be. We are mùirn beatha dàns. We are meant to be together."

But she wouldn't hear of it. She went on and on, scourging herself with guilt. Angus had been so good to her, so patient and kind. How could she hurt him this way? What we were doing was wrong, immoral, a betrayal of the worst kind.

"What about betraying our love?" I asked. "You've been perfectly willing to do that these last three years." I explained that I'd given up my life in Scotland. My family, my coven, they were no longer a part of me. I was here in America prepared to start my life over with her. What more could she want from me?

"I can't live with you and live with myself," she said. She fled the field like a frightened rabbit, she who was once destined to be high priestess of Belwicket.

"Well, I can't watch you live with Angus," I shouted at her fleeing form.

So tell me, Maeve, now that you've chosen a course I can't forgive, what is the value of your life?

—Neimhidh

With Ciaran gone from the room, the owl took over. "The rites must continue," she said.

They started their chanting again. I felt the dark energy building, the summoning of the purple-black light that would take my magick from me. And there was nothing I could do to stop it. I was completely outmatched.

I thought about Hunter. How much I loved him. How he was about to lose his life for me. How he was my *mùirn beatha dàn* and I'd known it all along but had never let myself embrace that truth. And I'd had the nerve to criticize Bree.

A world of regret rose up inside me. Regret for everything I'd done wrong.

I'd never told my parents how much I appreciated them. They'd given me a wonderful home and all their love, and when I'd found out I was adopted, all of that had seemed insignificant. Because of me, Mary K. had been kidnapped. Because of me, Cal was dead. He'd given his life for me and I'd wasted it completely.

Because of me, Hunter was going to die. That was the hardest thing of all.

My mind was spinning. I'd been alive only a little over seventeen years. How had I managed to make such a complete disaster of everything? The purple-black light crackled around me, and I thought, Take my power. Take my life. You're welcome to it.

Well, I'll drink a toast to you, Maeve Riordan. You pulled one over on me from beyond the grave. You were so young and beautiful when you died. I daresay you wouldn't find me attractive now. My own reflection stares back at me from this silver goblet, distorted, gruesome. How did I ever get such a beauty to love me, even for a night? Look at my eyes, two dark muddy slashes unlike anyone else's . . . except this girl's.

What do you think, Maeve? You know me better than most, so answer the question that looms before me: Can I now destroy our daughter?

The purple-black light surrounded the inner circle, holding me fast. The masked Amyranth witches stood in a circle around me, murmuring their chant.

I couldn't even control my own muscles. I tried to cast my senses to see just how much my tormentors were enjoying the show. But by now I was too weak even to do that.

The cougar held up a hand, and with a dull horror I saw that a cat's curved claws were growing from human fingertips. He muttered an incantation. The purple-black light crackled loudly and shot through my chest. I felt it wrap around my heart, squeezing mercilessly.

The magick was ebbing out of me. I felt it leaving. I didn't want to give in to Amyranth, to Ciaran's coven. I didn't want to let go of my magick. But I was so very tired of fighting. I felt the last bit of my resistance float away, and I followed it.

"Morgan, come back!" It was Hunter's voice. A hallucination, I told myself, and slipped back into the fog.

"No! I won't let you go. Not like this."

I forced my eyes open. Hunter stood in the doorway. A new aura of power seemed to flicker around him, his own sapphire light tinged with a purplish glow I'd never seen before.

Was he really there? How had he gotten away from Ciaran? Where was Ciaran? I couldn't imagine that Hunter had single-handedly overcome such evil. It had to be a dream.

"Seeker." The viper advanced on him.

Not a dream. My heart leaped wildly in my chest.

The weasel hurled a ball of blue witch light at Hunter. It found its target, and Hunter gasped in pain.

I struggled to pull myself out of the deadening fog. Hunter. I had to help him. Mentally I began my draw-power chant again. *An di allaigh* . . .

Power stirred inside me, faint as a hummingbird's heartbeat. But there.

In my mind I sang the chant again and again until I felt a

thin, steady stream of magick pouring into me. And then I sent it all to Hunter. *Help him,* I charged it. *Make him stronger. Heal his wounds.*

Hunter blocked a blow from the jackal, then turned and shot me a quick look of gratitude. I love you, Hunter, I thought. You've got to survive this.

Then Hunter chanted a spell in a language I didn't recognize. The fine garnet inlays on the table began to shudder. I watched wide-eyed as their forms rose into the air, glowing with the bloodred light of the gems. They were sigils, I realized. Hunter was calling them up.

The masked witches moved away from him, and I felt their terror. "Impossible," one murmured. "There's no way a Seeker could know how to use those sigils."

How did he do it? I wondered with distant amazement. Could the council really make him that much stronger? He seemed practically invincible.

The witch in the bear mask charged Hunter, but the witch never made it. He let out a sickening scream as he hit one of the glowing red sigils. He crashed to the floor, where the sigil ate at him the way fire ants devour a body.

And then Hunter was at my side, his athame out, its blade slicing through the spelled ropes that bound me. I felt him lift me from the table, murmur, "Thank God you're still alive."

"Hunter, no," I whispered. "Save yourself."

"Shhh," he whispered. "It's all right."

But the fog was washing over me, drawing me under again. And this time I let it take me.

*   *   *

Time had passed, I don't know how much. There was only Hunter and me, and we were on the sidewalk. He set me on my feet gently. "Do you think you can walk?" he asked.

"Yes," I said, though I was still terribly weak. Then Hunter was pulling me away from the house.

We got as far as the Museum of Natural History, where we both collapsed on the steps. It was dark and cold, and our breath came out in little clouds of vapor.

"Are you all right?" Hunter asked.

"I think so. My power . . . they didn't take it."

"No," he said softly. "You fought off an entire coven of Woodbanes. Thank the Goddess. I was nearly out of my mind with fright for you."

That was when I started to cry, great, gulping sobs that felt like they'd never stop.

Hunter folded me into his arms and held me. For a long time I stayed there in the shelter of his arms, crying until I had no more tears. Even after I stopped crying, I stayed there, listening to the steady sound of his heart, thinking it incredibly precious.

"I must be a mess," I said, finally breaking away to blow my nose. That's when I noticed Hunter's face was as tear-streaked as mine. "Hunter?" I asked uncertainly. "Are you okay?"

He nodded. "I'd better send a message to Sky, let everyone know we're all right." He concentrated for a moment, and I knew the message was being sent. "Here," he said then, taking off his jacket and draping it over my shoulders.

"How did you find me?" I asked. "I called you, but I got no answer. Ciaran was blocking my messages." I shuddered.

"I finally found Ciaran's ex-lover, and she told me where the coven was," Hunter explained.

"What happened to the Amyranth witches?" I asked.

"Still in the house. Recovering, I imagine. I hit them pretty hard, but I don't think I did much permanent damage," Hunter said. "I was more concerned with getting you out alive."

"But they're still there."

"Yes. I've sent a message to the council, but I doubt they'll get there before Amyranth clears out of that house. They'll surface again, though," he added grimly.

A kid came up to us, clutching a fistful of individually wrapped roses. "Hey, mister, want to buy a flower for the lady?" he asked.

Hunter stood up. "Yes, God, yes, I ought to buy her an entire bouquet, but"—he reached into his pocket and pulled out his billfold—"I'll take one. Keep the change."

"Thanks," the boy said, his face lighting up as he realized Hunter had given him a twenty.

"That was generous," I said as the boy ran off and Hunter dropped down beside me again.

He shrugged. "I'm feeling generous and grateful—and phenomenally sorry. So much more than sorry." He handed me the flower. "Morgan, I don't know how to apologize."

"For what? You don't have anything to apologize for," I protested. "I'm the one who charged in there like the Mounties to the rescue."

He gave me that stern Hunter look. "You did, and remind me to give you a hard time for it someday, but the truth is—this was all my fault."

I snuggled closer. "How do you figure that?"

"Isn't it obvious? I should have realized Amyranth wanted you."

"Stop blaming yourself," I told him. I ran my hand along his smooth cheek. He was so dear to me. "It was the council who got it totally wrong. How could they have thought the target was Ciaran's child?"

Hunter didn't say anything.

"I guess I shouldn't blame them," I added grudgingly. "I mean, I did see myself as a wolf cub in the dream. But obviously that didn't mean what we all assumed it meant."

Hunter gazed at me with an expression of pity and grief. "Oh, Morgan," he said. "I thought you already knew."

"Knew what?" Sudden, nameless dread lodged somewhere below my heart, a dark, cold mass.

"The dream meant exactly what we thought. The council didn't get it wrong. The target was Ciaran's child."

"But Killian was never their captive and—"

"Never mind Killian. There's one thing none of us knew," he interrupted, his voice gentle. "Not even Ciaran—until he did _tàth meànma_ on you. He saw Maeve holding you as an infant—and he heard what she said about your eyes. Morgan, Angus had blue eyes. Yours are brown . . . like your father's."

"No." I started to shake again as I understood what he was saying. "That can't be. It's impossible. I won't believe—"

Hunter put one hand on the side of my face. "Morgan, you _are_ Ciaran's child."

rejected me. The heart she would not accept from me, I gave to the darkness. My power has grown beyond what I ever believed possible. I have served the darkness well, and it me. There is nothing on this earth that frightens me and very little that can stand against me. Would the good witch of Belwicket be able to accept that? I must believe that our love would open her to her own true Woodbane nature and that she would revel in it as I do.

Meanwhile my love for her only grows. It never seems to diminish, no matter how I distract myself. I've tried everything, even stooping to childish tricks. I've left anonymous threatening sigils around their house. I've even hung a dead cat from their porch rail. Goddess, it's sickening, juvenile stuff, but I am a man possessed. What shall I do? What can I do?

—Neimhidh

I don't know how long I sat there on the steps of the museum, trying to wrap my mind around what Hunter had just told me. I was numb, unable to process it. It was too dark, too monstrous. I couldn't let it in.

Ciaran, my true father?

No. No, no, no. It simply couldn't be.

"Listen, love," Hunter said. "I want to tell you about him."

"Please. Don't." I couldn't say anything else. His jacket hung open on my shoulders. I wasn't even feeling the cold anymore.

"No, you need to hear this. It was Ciaran who freed me.

14

Tainted

May 25, 1985

I tried to forget her, I swear it. I returned to Scotland.
another go with Grania and the little ones, every bit as miser
as the other times. Killian is an interesting one, though. He
more innate power than Kyle and Iona combined. He could b
real find. Still, I can't share a roof with any of them, not w
it's Maeve I ache for. She's a craving in my heart, a sickness
my blood. I wake and fall asleep to her memory. I love her as m
as I hate her. She is with me every minute.

But the truth is, she remains with Angus, damn him. Time a
again I've tried to persuade her to leave the worthless fool. A
time and again she refuses.

I wonder sometimes what would be if she gave me a chan
if she saw who it is I've become in these years since she fir

He told me you were his daughter and that I had to save you."

"Why? So he can drain me again?" I said.

Hunter sighed. "You're not listening. Ciaran gave me the spell for calling up the sigils in the table. And he added his power to mine. Don't you know I couldn't have held off all those witches on my own? Neither one of us would have gotten out of there alive without his help. Morgan, whatever he is, whatever he's done, he couldn't kill you. Not his own child."

"It doesn't matter," I replied dully. "He's still evil. A murderer. And I'm his daughter." Robbie had been right about me. I was fundamentally tainted. It was my birthright.

"Morgan—"

I put my finger to Hunter's lips. "Stop. Please. If there's one thing I've learned from all this, it's that you can't change what's fated to be."

Hunter rubbed his temple. "We need to talk about this, but tonight's obviously not the right time."

"We should get out of the city," I said with a shudder. "Before Amyranth regroups. Let's go get everyone. I'll drive back to Widow's Vale tonight."

Hunter gave a hollow laugh. "I'm not even sure you're capable of climbing into a cab, much less driving upstate. No, we'll spend the night in the city. I expect we'll be safe enough. But first thing tomorrow morning we'll get the hell out."

He hailed a cab and helped me into it.

It was late when we got back to the apartment. We rode up in the elevator in silence. It was only when we got out on Bree's floor that I realized I was still wearing that awful brown robe. "How am I going to explain this?" I asked.

Hunter brushed a strand of hair out of my face. "It's after eleven. Maybe they'll all be asleep."

They were. Sky and Raven were in the living room, nestled together on the pullout couch. Raven looked content, peaceful, almost innocent.

I found a note from Bree on the kitchen counter.

> M&H—
>
> I'm so glad you're all right! Since my dad is still in Connecticut, Robbie and I are camping out in the master bedroom. You guys can take the guest room.
> —B

In tiny print at the bottom she'd added another note: *M— You were right about me. How about that?*

Hunter was standing at the closed door of the guest room. "Morgan, look," he said softly. On the doorknob Bree had hung a small wreath wound through with white blossoms. Their sweet, heady scent filled the hallway. "Jasmine," Hunter said with a smile. "Wonder where she found it at this time of year?" He took my hand. "Shall we go in?"

I tried to force a smile, but I couldn't.

"Hunter," I began, my voice breaking, "I don't know how to say this, but—I just hurt a lot right now. I need to sleep on my own tonight."

I saw the flash of pain in Hunter's eyes and felt a remote sense of guilt, of regret. Here, at last, was our chance to spend a whole night together. After surviving the disaster at Ciaran's, sleeping together was exactly what should have followed, a natural way to ground ourselves in life again after having come so close to death. An affirmation of our love, a time for comfort. But I couldn't accept it. Not now.

"If that's what you need . . ." Hunter's voice trailed off.

"It is." I reached up and touched his cheek. "Thanks. For everything."

"Anytime," he said.

I walked into the guest room and caught sight of my reflection in the mirror. For the space of several heartbeats I forced myself to study my own face. My cheeks were tear-streaked, my nose slightly swollen. My eyes were puffy and red. And exactly the same shape and color as Ciaran's.

I felt a sick appreciation for the irony of it. After all these years I finally knew who I resembled.

I couldn't look anymore. I needed a shower desperately, but I was too tired. The shower would wait until morning. I stripped off the brown robe. In the morning I'd stuff it down the garbage chute.

I went into the guest room and climbed into bed. I closed my eyes and willed sleep, but an endless tape kept running through my head: Ciaran is my father. Ciaran is my father. Ciaran is my father.

I couldn't doubt it. Not after the connection I'd felt with him. Not after I'd looked in the mirror and seen his eyes staring out from my face.

My father was a murderer, the leader of a Woodbane coven whose purpose was to destroy other covens. He'd killed Maeve and Angus. He was pure evil.

It occurred to me that Killian was my half brother.

All sorts of things began to fall into place. Things that

hadn't quite made sense before. The sense of connection I'd felt with Ciaran—and with Killian. My unusual powers. Not only was I heir to Belwicket's legacy of magick, but to Ciaran's as well. And my own tendency to abuse power definitely came from Ciaran.

Through the wall I heard Hunter curse the couch in the study. Bree had told me that it was lumpy and uncomfortable.

Tears leaked from the corners of my eyes. I loved Hunter in a way I'd never loved anyone. But I couldn't be with him. Not now, knowing what I really was.

An heir to darkness.

15

Broken

June 1985

I am back in Meshomah Falls now so I can put an end to it once and for all. There will be no more fevers, no more senseless cravings. No more pining for a woman who won't have me. I'm choosing my own peace of mind over all else. Giving in to the inevitable.

If she wants Angus so badly, let her have him for eternity. Let them both die. I've found the perfect place for it, an isolated barn on an abandoned farm about five miles from their house. The means will be Maeve's own element, fire. It seems the only fitting thing. A fire to quench the fire that's been burning in my heart since the day I first saw her.

Fire to fire and ashes to ashes. It will soon be done. I've already closed my heart to love. From this day on I give myself wholly to the darkness.

—Neimhidh

We were back in Widow's Vale by noon on Monday. After I dropped everyone off, I finally drove back to my own house. My parents' cars were both gone, and I didn't see any lights on inside. I cast my senses. No one home except Dagda.

I knew I should go in and unpack, hug my kitten, but somehow I wasn't ready. Instead I pulled out of the driveway again and drove to the road that runs along the Hudson River.

I turned in at the marina parking lot. The town has a dock there where small boats tie up in the summer. In the winter it's deserted, just a crescent of stony beach and a rough wooden dock jutting out into the water.

It was terribly cold, but I didn't care. I needed the solitude. The river, an expanse of silver-gray beneath white winter skies, was calm and seemed infinitely peaceful. I walked to the end of the dock. Despite the snows we'd had, the water level was a good six feet below the dock, so I sat on the end and dangled my feet.

This river flows to New York City, I thought. This river connects the two places, rising and falling with the tides of the Atlantic. I'd been feeling relatively safe since returning to Widow's Vale, but the silver-gray waters reminded me that New York and Widow's Vale were linked, part of a whole. What I'd left in the city would always be part of my life.

Like Ciaran. My natural father. I was still struggling with the implications of that revelation. How was I going to use my magick, knowing that half my power came from Ciaran? Just the thought of magick gave me a sick, hollow feeling.

As for love . . . I'd barely been able to stand the car ride back home. It felt like torture to sit next to Hunter, knowing what had to come next.

I had to break up with him. I just hadn't been able to summon the strength that morning.

It all came down to Ciaran. My biological father wasn't good, kind Angus. My father was a man who'd murdered his own *mùirn beatha dàn*. A man who'd sucked the power and the life from who knew how many innocent people. And if he was capable of those crimes, then what crimes was I, his daughter, his own flesh and blood, capable of committing?

I'd already made so many mistakes that cost me and others dearly. I'd had terrible judgment. I'd trusted Cal, Selene, David, and Ciaran. I'd hurt Bree, nearly killed Hunter—twice now—and watched Cal die for me. I'd almost driven Robbie away. I'd caused my parents pain. I'd put Mary K.'s life in terrible danger. Two and a half months of magick and I was a walking minefield.

And all because of what I was. Like father, like daughter. I was poison. Everyone I touched was tainted by me.

I felt a surge of despair as my senses began to tingle. Hunter was nearby. I heard the sound of his beat-up old Honda driving down the winding path to the water. I guessed I couldn't put it off after all.

Moments later Hunter got out of his car. He was wearing a long, straight navy wool coat that made him look formal and grown up. His hair framed his face in a halo of gold. I'd forgotten how sometimes it seemed like he was made of sunlight.

Whereas I was the heir to darkness.

He walked up to me cautiously. "Am I intruding?"

"Sort of," I said honestly. "I came here because I needed time alone."

"Want me to leave?"

I shook my head. I didn't want him to leave. I wanted to run into his arms, hold him, and never let him go.

We stared at each other while I tried to find the words to say the impossible.

"I wanted you to know," he said. "I just got word on Killian. Apparently he thought the owl was sent to spy on him, as we all did. He took off, fearing that Amyranth really was after him. He's still lying low, but I just got word that he's okay."

"Oh," I said dully. "That's good."

Hunter's green eyes studied me. "Killian may be okay," he said slowly. "You, on the other hand, clearly are not."

"You noticed," I said, trying to sound a whole lot cooler than I felt.

"Of course I noticed," he said, looking at me as intensely as ever. "What do you take me for?"

I felt frozen, unable to speak.

He ran a hand through his hair and said in a gentler tone, "Morgan, tell me what I can do. How can I help?"

"I—" My voice died in my throat. I couldn't say it. It hurt too much. "You can't," I got out at last. "No one can."

I thought of what it felt like to lie in Hunter's arms, to laugh with him, to join my power with his. How could I give up any of that? There would never be anyone who felt that right, never anyone I would love that much, ever again. He was my soul mate.

"All right." He shoved his hands into his coat pockets as if to keep himself from touching me. "Maybe you're not ready to talk right now. Can we get together tomorrow night?"

"No!" I said more forcefully than I'd meant to.

"Why not?"

I thought again of how I'd hurt everyone who came near me. How as Ciaran's daughter, I couldn't possibly do anything else.

"I guess I need to get used to it," I said finally.

"Used to what?"

"To what it's going to be like without you." My voice sounded hollow and alien, like it was coming out of someone else's body.

"What?" He let out a sharp, startled bark of laughter. "What are you saying?"

I couldn't look at him. "I have to be on my own. I'm poison, Hunter. I can't help it."

Hunter blew out his breath, a cloud of steam in the icy air. "Don't be ridiculous. Heritage does not equal destiny."

"For me it does. I can't be with you anymore. We have to break up."

There. It was out. I shut my eyes tight against the pain. It was worse than anything I'd experienced at the hands of Amyranth. I felt like I'd just cut out my own heart.

"We have to do what?" Hunter's voice was carefully controlled, as if he were trying to convince himself he'd misheard me.

"I'm breaking up with you," I said more strongly. I opened my eyes, but I still couldn't look at him. I stared at the wooden slats of the dock below my feet and wondered what it would be like to drop through them, sink into the frigid water below. Don't cry, Morgan. You will not cry. I took a deep breath and said the only thing I could think of that would make him go away. "I don't love you anymore."

"Really?" His voice was like ice. "When did that happen?"

"Things—things have changed," I said, trying to keep my voice steady. "I'm sorry. I just don't love you anymore."

Hunter just looked at me. We both knew I was lying.

"Listen." His voice was ragged. "I came here to tell you something else. I never really believed in all this *mùirn beatha dàn* stuff. I thought it was just romantic nonsense. But Morgan, you are my *mùirn beatha dàn*. I realized that when I thought I was going to lose you to Amyranth. I love you—absolutely, totally, forever. Know that."

Oh, God. It hurt so much, the words I'd been waiting for, words that should have made me so happy. And all I could think was: Don't tell me that now. Please. You can't love me.

"Look at me, dammit." Hunter was inches away from me now. "Look at me and tell me you want to break up."

I raised my eyes to his and saw pain and grief and confusion—and love. No one would ever look at me with that much love again. I blinked back tears. "I want to break up."

"Oh, Morgan," he said. Then he took that final step toward me, and somehow our arms were around each other. He held me while I cried, and I could feel both our hearts breaking.

"I love you," he said again, which only made me cry harder.

I don't know how long we stood together like that. When we finally stepped apart, the front of his wool coat was spongy with my tears.

"I have to go now," I told him. "Don't call me." Before either of us could say more, I turned and ran toward Das Boot. The wind rose, howling down the river, echoing our pain. But Hunter's voice managed to carry over it.

"We make our own choices," he called after me.

F
TIE

Tiernan, Cate.

The calling.

51795

$7.99

DATE			